MENTAL

By

Poppy Brunel

DEDICATION

For my children.
I love you. Always.

CONTENTS

ACKNOWLEDGMENTS

Oodles of love, hugs and thanks to my three children for being my inspiration and the most supportive siblings. Thank you to my lovely friend for sharing your innermost feelings and experiences with me. You know who you are!

AUTHOR'S NOTE

Mental is a fictional book. The characters, the schools and the specific services mentioned are all fictional. However, Samuel's experiences are based on my son's personal adventure with ADHD, and the words in the prologue are his own. Thank you to my children for teaching me so much and making my life so colourful.

Amelia is not based on myself, but my emotions and struggles around supporting a child with ADHD are very much woven into Amelia's character.

Thank you to my anonymous friend for sharing her personal story about how her depression affects her daily. You helped Amelia come alive. I couldn't have written this without you.

PART ONE

Prologue

'I'm a very special boy. I must be special because so many people help me. That makes me special, doesn't it? They never want to leave me on my own, so I am really, really special. I think I'm special because I have lots of problems. Some of the other children have problems too. It isn't just me. They're special, too.

'Sometimes school is too hard. I love school, but it can make me feel strange. They make me do a lot of choosing. Choosing is when I can only do, say, fifteen sums, but the other children do more. I get to do choosing when they do their sums. I can paint or go outside or play the piano. Because if I do more than fifteen sums, I will explode. Boom! All over the walls. What do you think I would look like over the walls? Do you think it would be messy? Would the other children still do their sums then? Some of them can do, like, one hundred and twenty-eight sums. How do they do that without exploding?

'When I feel like I am about to explode it's because I have done too much. Too much maths. Too much writing. Too much sitting. Because it's like I have a number my brain can get to. My brain only goes up to one hundred. If I do one sum I am at number ten in my brain. If I do fourteen sums I am at ninety-nine in my brain. Fifteen sums goes up to one hundred. I am OK until I get to one hundred. If I get to one hundred and one then I explode. When I am writing I get to one hundred after one paragraph. The other children can write five paragraphs and still not be at one hundred. I don't know why.

'When I explode, my brain leaves my head. It goes *whoosh* and I can feel it go. And then my heart goes *whoosh* and it goes too. Then I can feel it over my whole body. In my fingers, in my legs, in my ears, in my eyes, in my head – everywhere. It feels all weird and it hurts. You know when you hurt yourself? If you bang your leg? Ow, ow, ow! I feel it everywhere when I get to one hundred. And then I have to run away because it feels horrible. I keep running and running and running. Run out of school! Run out of school! When they touch me, it hurts.

'I can't stop it. I can feel it coming, and I know it's coming, but I can't stop it. I get all stressed because I can feel it coming. You can't stop it either, Mummy. I have to wait for it to stop. It makes me thirsty. And I get scared. I get so scared.'

Chapter 1

September 2011

It was half past seven and time to leave for school. Two pairs of brand-new, beautifully polished school shoes were standing to attention in the hall, waiting for their first adventure of many. Mia and Samuel looked immaculate in their new uniforms, and they were running around the house, laughing, with an air of excitement and anticipation.

'Come on, then. Shoes on,' I said.

I wished I could share even an ounce of their excitement, but all I felt was dread, panic, nerves and a slightly nauseous feeling which wouldn't go away, no matter how much I scolded myself for it. It was Mia and Samuel's first day of school.

'I'm very excited, Mummy,' Samuel said, whilst chewing on his sleeve.

I studied his face. Yes, I could see the excitement, dancing behind his eyes. But I could also see the nerves, too. His eyes darted around a little too quickly. He chewed his sleeve a little too insistently. He twirled around and around a little too ferociously.

My heart heaved, and I wished I could make it all go away. Whose stupid idea was it to send four-year-olds to school? They should be going on bear hunts, splashing in puddles, baking cookies and swinging high at the park. With me. Their mummy. Not a teacher who had never met them before.

Who would cuddle them when they cried? Who would sing their favourite songs, whilst twirling their hair, when they got scared? Who would hold their hands when they needed that extra bit of emotional support? Who would notice when Samuel got that look of panic when the wind blew too noisily? Who would help them get their shoes onto the right feet and remind them to wash their hands after going to the toilet?

It should have been me. And that broke my heart.

On top of the pain of sending the twins to school for the first time, there were a few other factors giving the day extra levels of uncertainty, angst and guilt. Having stayed at home with my children whilst they were too young for school, I was now going back to work full-time. And it was my first day too, as an English teacher in the local secondary school. As a consequence of this, on Mia and Samuel's first day at school, they were attending the breakfast club there. Oh, the guilt connected with not being able to walk my children into the classroom on their first day of school. I would be replaced by a breakfast club member of staff. How could I do that to them, as their mum? It should have been me.

Their dad Ben had died years ago. We had been married for five years and he was my world. The sudden news that he had terminal cancer had secretly destroyed me, although I tried not to show it in front of Ben, and he died not long after his tragic diagnosis. The twins were just a few months old. I had initially thought that I would drown from the grief, but the twins had managed to save me. They still needed me, every second of the day, and wallowing in despair became impossible. So, I learnt to cope. There was no other choice.

I managed to keep our pretty little two-bedroom, terraced house, thanks to Ben's insurance money, and we gradually rebuilt our lives. For four years the twins and I had been inseparable, but that was all about to end.

I hated myself as I drove them up to the gate. Hated myself as I said goodbye, with a forced smile firmly in place, wishing the children a day of sunshine, light and happiness. A glance over my shoulder as I got to the door, just in time to see tears brimming in Samuel's eyes.

I wanted to run back. Hold him. Take them both away. Grab our wellies and go puddle-splashing before stopping for a picnic of jam sandwiches. They were too little for school. And I wasn't ready.

I made it out of the door before the hot tears flowed freely down my face. Avoiding eye contact with any other parents outside the gates, I reached my car with relief and rested my head on the cool steering wheel as I allowed myself to sob.

Time was ticking on, however, and my new job

awaited. It felt unfair. If I couldn't whisk my children far away from school, then I wanted to lie in my bed and eat cookie-dough ice cream instead; counting down the minutes until it was time to collect them. But I couldn't.

Turning the key in the ignition and wiping my eyes carefully to avoid smudging my damp make-up, I drove through the Suffolk countryside towards my new job, already feeling drained of energy.

It was the first day of the rest of our lives. I wasn't ready. But things could only get easier.

*

It took just two weeks. Two weeks into the new school year, and the reception class teacher, Miss Farnham, was waiting for me after school.

'Miss May? Can I have a quick word, please?'

Taken by surprise, I wasn't expecting to be called into school. *It's OK*, I thought. *It's just to show me some work. Or go over the new reading books. Maybe I haven't done enough reading at home with the twins?*

A touch of neurosis crept up on me, making my heart pound. What had they done? Samuel was sitting on a chair in the corner, swinging his legs energetically. Upon seeing me, he ran across the room.

'Mummy, Mummy, Mummy…'

'Sit back down, Samuel, I need to speak to your mum,' said his teacher. Her tone was clipped and irate. I looked at her in surprise and welcomed Samuel's embrace. *How dare she snap at him like that?* I thought. He clung to me more tightly than usual.

'He's fine here with me,' I answered, lifting Samuel

onto my hip. He rested his head on my shoulder and I stroked his soft, blond curls. Mia then appeared, beaming as she ran over to me. I gave her a quick hug and guided her onto the chair next to me.

'Samuel has not had a good week. He refuses to sit on the carpet with the other children, can't wait his turn for the computers and makes loud noises whilst the rest of the class are silent. He won't participate in phonics sessions and prefers to just run around the classroom. When it is time for break, he refuses to go outside, and then once he does go outside, he won't come back in. Samuel refuses to conform.'

Refuses to conform? He had been at school for just two weeks, and he refused to conform? Surely this was a joke. If he was having trouble adjusting to being in a class of thirty children, then was it not the job of the school to ease him into this effectively? Was it not their responsibility to develop his skills to enable him to understand the rules of the classroom and engage in all activities? Or was I missing something?

Should I have prepared him better? *Could* I have prepared him better? But how? Maybe I should have sent him to a bigger, more structured nursery. Maybe I should have practised sitting on a carpet whilst being read to, as opposed to on my lap. Maybe I should have been stricter with the activities that he did at home: changing them at any given time against his will and not allowing him his own free choice of toys and games.

No, no, no – he's four! The idea of enforcing restrictions connected to his playtime at home seemed ludicrous. So, what could I have done to prepare him better for school? My mind drew a blank. This wasn't my fault.

'What are you doing to help Samuel adjust to the new classroom routine?' I asked.

'The same as for all of the other children. They are all given clear instructions, and gentle reminders, but Samuel is the only child who still will not conform.'

I stared at her, stunned.

'Samuel's behaviour isn't acceptable. Please could you reinforce at home our behaviour policy to assist us in the classroom?' she said.

No words came. I nodded my head feebly and turned towards the door, still holding Samuel tightly and gripping Mia's hand. I never wanted to return to that classroom. I never wanted to do that to my son again. What had I done wrong? Why was he different? Why was he struggling?

But he was just four.

The teacher called over to us wearily. 'Bye, Samuel. Be good for your mum.'

Samuel screamed loudly.

He's just four.

Chapter 2

October 2011

Half-term had felt just out of reach for so long. As the weeks slowly passed we painfully dragged ourselves towards the finishing line using our fingernails, watching them rip off one by one with the effort needed to get to our final destination. We were nearly there.

My little chats with Samuel's teacher had become a twice-weekly occurrence. The other three days a week had offered gentle and welcome respite as the children attended after-school club whilst I worked. What a relief those three days had become.

Samuel still couldn't conform. He was unable to articulate why – which was hardly surprising considering his age. However, one thing had become clear: he was getting worse.

'Samuel screams during class... Samuel hasn't made any friends... Samuel is unable to play nicely with the other children… Samuel never completes his work… Samuel chooses to stay outside the classroom… Samuel spends most of the day on a chair which he has taken into the cloakroom…'

My heart broke on a daily basis with trying to understand his unease in the classroom. Why couldn't he manage it? Every time, the teacher asked me to remind Samuel of the school rules and expectations. He knew them, though. He just couldn't do it.

Mia, on the other hand, had settled into school life with ease, and had made many friends. Her work was above average and I was told that she was friendly and polite throughout the day. I would feel waves of relief, knowing that I couldn't have messed up my parenting too much if Mia was so settled.

I approached the school gates with the usual trepidation, waiting for the teacher's welcome. But she was nowhere to be seen. With a sigh of relief, I entered the classroom.

The head teacher, Mrs Baxter, was waiting for me.

'Could you come to the library please, Miss May? Your children are there, waiting for you.'

Oh God.

I nodded and followed her through the classroom and into the library where Mia and Samuel were sitting on bean-bags, looking at books. They came running over to greet me, and I sank down to the floor to hold them.

'You both OK?' I asked, eyebrows raised.

'Well, Samuel's in trouble again,' Mia replied, matter-of-factly.

'I'm not, I'm not,' Samuel said. He buried his face in my hair, and I held him, sighing.

'Samuel has committed a very serious offence today. He bit his teacher. She is very upset and has taken the afternoon off to recover,' Mrs Baxter said.

I felt sick. 'What? Why? Why did he bite her?'

'It was completely unprovoked. There doesn't appear to be any reason why he would have done this. To make matters worse, he has shown no remorse whatsoever.'

'I don't believe that for one minute. He bit her for no reason? Have you asked Samuel why he did it?' My voice was starting to shake with the emotion that had suddenly erupted from within.

'Samuel has just been squealing and shrieking ever since. I brought him straight here for the rest of the afternoon.'

A quiet, high pitched whimper emanated from somewhere within my hair. I sat on the floor and pulled Samuel onto my lap.

'Did something happen, Sammy? What happened?'

The whimpering continued and his grasp around my neck tightened. At that moment, Miss Farnham appeared through the library door. Her face looked drawn and pale, and her arms were firmly crossed. I tried to get eye contact with her, but she defiantly looked the other way.

'I'm sorry Samuel bit you. Can you tell me why?'

She carried on looking the other way, refusing to answer, and I could feel anger growing inside. I wanted to shout at her. Surely this couldn't have been the first time a child in reception had lashed out? Was my son really the first child to have ever bit someone in the classroom? Were all the other children little angels or what?

Mrs Baxter spoke for Miss Farnham. 'Miss Farnham had asked all of the children to sit on the carpet in a circle. Samuel chose a chair instead and sat behind the circle. Miss Farnham simply held on to Samuel to guide him onto the carpet, and he bit her. It was unprovoked.'

'Unprovoked? But you have been telling me twice a week all term that Samuel is unable to sit on the carpet with the other children. Surely, the reason for him not feeling able to sit with the other children needs addressing first before being physically forced to sit with them? That's why he bit Miss Farnham. Isn't that obvious?'

'Miss Farnham was very gentle. He was not pulled off his chair. She put her arm around Samuel to guide him to the floor, and he bit her arm.'

'Of course he bit her arm! She put her arm around him to make him sit on the floor. You've told me many times that he struggles to sit on the floor with the children. Have you tried to address *why* he struggles before enforcing it on him?'

'Well, he could be autistic,' Mrs Baxter said, simply. A throwaway comment that lingered in the air for just a moment before thumping me in the stomach with the force of a boxing glove.

Wait. What?

Autism. Such a scary word. I had never even considered this. *Could he have autism? No. No, not Samuel.*

Could he?

'OK,' I said, slowly. 'If he has autism, then forcibly making him sit with the other children is a little cruel, don't you think? Making him conform is also cruel. So, how do you suggest we proceed from here?'

There was silence in the library, except for Mia playing quietly. I looked from the head teacher's pointed, spiky face to the pale and weary reception teacher who was markedly staring out of the window. Something in my little world had just changed, and I wasn't prepared for it.

Mrs Baxter informed me that she would be requesting an assessment for autism and would be needing me to come into school to help complete the paperwork. In shock, I quietly bundled Samuel up into my arms and called over to Mia. We left under a cloud of awkward hostility; my repeated apology to Miss Farnham was left drifting in the air as she again chose to not respond.

Autism?

Not Samuel. Not my baby boy.

Chapter 3

December 2011

Mia and I ran out of the school, hand in hand, giggling as if we had just successfully broken out of prison. Freedom! No work or school all afternoon because Mia had an eye appointment at the hospital. These had been a regular occurrence over the past year since I discovered – with a huge amount of surprise – just how bad her eyesight was. This, of course, brought the usual barrage of Mum Guilt. How could I have not known that she couldn't see properly?

The optician had not initially helped my guilt. In fact, he had helped to fuel it further.

'Did you not realise that she couldn't see very clearly? She needs a strong prescription.'

No, I hadn't realised, but thank you for rubbing that so liberally in to the already open and oozing wounds of my self-confidence as a parent.

Mia had never been able to see anything

particularly well, but she had nothing to compare her vision to so thought it was normal. She didn't squint, or move closer to objects to see them better, so I had no reason to believe that she couldn't see clearly.

The trip to the hospital was always something to look forward to. Life was always so hectic, and it hardly ever allowed me time with just one of my children, so it was a time to be treasured. Even if it was just an afternoon at the hospital. Mia and I held hands and swung each other's arms happily as we crossed the carpark.

'Will I get to choose new glasses today?' Mia asked.

'Possibly. Do you know what colour you want to get?'

'Pink! They have to be pink. Or purple. Will I need to have the drops?'

'I don't know, sweetie.'

'I don't want to. I don't like the drops.'

'I know.' I squeezed her hand, wishing – not for the first time – that I could take her place. The drops stung her eyes and left her feeling disorientated as her pupils expanded. I didn't want her to have them, either.

*

The waiting room was quiet. Mia made her way over to the toy box and busied herself immediately, investigating every toy within its colourful and noisy depths. I went to join her but a ringing in my bag distracted me.

'Damn, I meant to turn that off.'

Reaching in my bag, I noticed the caller ID

illuminated on my screen. *School.*

'I've got to answer this, Mia. You OK for a minute?'

'Yes, Mummy.'

I left the waiting area and stood just outside the door, watching Mia through the glass panel, and hurriedly answered the call.

'Miss May?'

'Yes.'

'Good afternoon, it's Mrs Baxter here.'

The head teacher. Why would she be calling me?

'I'm sorry to report that we have had an unfortunate incident at school this afternoon. Samuel has bitten another child. I am left with no choice but to exclude him from school until Thursday morning.'

Exclude him? That couldn't be right.

'I thought that you were under the assumption that Samuel has autism? How can you exclude him for reacting to another child if it is due to something like autism?'

Panic and anger merged inside me, making my heart beat more quickly and my voice sound breathless. How could Samuel be excluded from school?

'Whether Samuel is autistic or not, biting is not acceptable.'

'Even if he is unable to understand proper social etiquette with his classmates? Is it still unacceptable?' Clutching at straws, I could feel myself pleading with her to see sense. Samuel wasn't a naughty boy. He couldn't be excluded.

'I'm sorry, but this is my decision. He is ready to be collected now if you can come into school.'

Pleading turned to pure anger. 'You know exactly where I am right now. I collected Mia for a hospital appointment. Are you expecting me to neglect my daughter's health and walk away from the hospital before she has had a chance to be seen?'

'Please don't raise your voice, Miss May. You must collect Samuel as soon as you are able.'

'He can't stay at home tomorrow. I have to work. I took today off to take Mia to her appointment. I can't take a second day off.'

'That isn't my problem. Samuel needs to be collected as soon as possible, and he is not to come back to school until Thursday morning. You will be expected to be at a meeting to discuss this at nine o'clock on Thursday morning.'

'I'll be working at nine on Thursday! What's this supposed to achieve? Samuel isn't going to see a day at home as a punishment. He's going to be happy he doesn't have to put up with your school for a day, and he gets to be with Mum. That's not a punishment.'

'Ah, but it is. He'll miss the trip to the theatre tomorrow.'

And there it was. Realisation suddenly started to trickle into my thoughts.

'I know why you've done this. You told me that you were worried about taking Samuel on the coach to the theatre. You've managed to get out of it! How convenient for you.'

'I can assure you that is not the reason, Miss May.

What time will you be collecting Samuel, please?'

'At the end of the school day. I'm with Mia right now.'

I hung up without saying goodbye. Tears prickled under my eyelids, and I angrily wiped them away before going back to Mia.

How ethical was it to exclude a child for behaving in a way that he didn't seem to be in control of? Was it acceptable? I just didn't know. Maybe I should have questioned Mrs Baxter further. I doubted it would have made any difference, however. School had ensured that the *naughty boy* label had been tattooed onto Samuel's forehead and there didn't appear to be anything I could do or say to change their minds.

Chapter 4

January 2012

He came out of nowhere. A voice; somewhere on the internet. I was trying to organise an author to visit my students at school to motivate their creative writing. How convenient, then, that I knew an author of published young adult books. I met Robin at university. We had dated for a few weeks, but it was never very serious, and we drifted apart quite quickly. Thinking about him, all those years later, gave me a tingling in my stomach.

I wasn't really expecting Robin to answer. Why would he remember me after all those years?

Hey, Robin. Remember me? I was wondering if I could ask a favour, please? A. x

Why did I feel so nervous whilst writing those few words? Would he even remember who I was? University was a long time ago. My heart beat rapidly as I pressed send. The reply was almost instant.

Amelia! Of course I remember you! Fire away! x

Oh my god. He answered. Buzzing, I quickly replied.

I teach English now, and I am looking for an author to come and work with some of my students. Any chance you'd be interested? Or know someone who might be? Thanks. A. x

Again, the answer was almost straight away.

Sounds like fun. Do you use Skype? We can chat more easily. x

A ghost from my past, and suddenly I was sucked into this exciting, colourful web of love online. Robin lived in Swansea, so our long-distance relationship had its complications, and we hadn't yet met up. It had been two weeks since my first message, and we got carried away in a world consisting of constant texts and nightly Skype calls.

I hadn't noticed that I'd been lonely before. Maybe I hadn't been. Maybe I was actually content with life as it was, free from the emotional highs and lows that a relationship brought. Carefree with no additional pressures. Yet, since Robin had re-entered my life, I couldn't exist without him.

Unlocking my phone, a text was waiting.

Hey, sweetie. Missing you… xx

I answered, grinning inanely. *Missing you, too! So much. The day's dragged. You free to chat soon? Xx*

Just got a bit of writing to finish off then I'll jump on Skype. Half hour OK? Xx

No, that's too long ;) xx

I'll be as quick as I can, sweetie. Love you. xxxXXXxxx

Love you more. xXxXxXxXx

What started as friendly chat quickly evolved and blossomed into true love. Wales felt like a very long drive from Suffolk, however. It wasn't an ideal relationship. How could it possibly work? He spent most weekends with his ten-year-old daughter, Emily, from a previous marriage, which made it difficult to see him.

I wondered why he even bothered. What could the appeal be? Was I wasting his time? I didn't make him love me, though. He wanted to. He needed me. And I desperately needed him.

When we were online together everything else became still. The world stopped spinning. We existed in our own little bubble which carefully constructed itself around us. It was a beautiful and serene place to be.

Was it even a relationship if it existed purely online? I thought it must be. We spent three hours every night immersed in a Skype call with each other, and we shared everything together. He just wasn't there.

I wished he was.

My iPad started ringing as a Skype call came in. My heart leapt.

'Hello, you,' I said, as his face appeared on the screen. I caught my breath, surprising myself again with just how happy it made me to see him. He looked just as content, and his eyes sparkled.

'Hey. How are you?' he asked.

'I'm good, now.'

'I've got something I want to ask you.'

'OK,' I answered, expectantly.

'Firstly, an apology. Work has been mad, and I can't see it easing for the next few weeks. However, I'm desperate to see you and it's still over a month until I'm coming over to see your students. So, how about we meet halfway on Saturday night and stay in a hotel? Emily is away with her mum this weekend. Could you get childcare?'

'Yes. Definitely,' I said, before thinking. He laughed.

'Are you sure? What will you do with the children?'

'I have no idea, but I'll sort something. I have to see you.'

What *would* I do with them? Nobody was very forthcoming with babysitting both children overnight. Especially Samuel. He wasn't the easiest child to look after.

'Have any of your friends got teenage daughters who could come over for the night? I'll pay them,' he said.

'Maybe.' Racking my brain. There had to be someone. 'Yes! Annie's daughter is seventeen. I'll ask her.' I literally couldn't contain my excitement. I didn't care how I found a babysitter, but I would. I needed to see Robin.

*

To say that Samuel was playing up didn't even come close. Annie's daughter, Katie, was due over in an hour, and I hadn't even finished cooking their dinner. It had just been one thing after another, and I had seriously had enough. I wished it was time to see Robin.

Earlier, Samuel had drawn on the wall. Why would he do that? He knew that it wasn't acceptable. Then, Samuel tipped his entire Lego collection all over the lounge floor, upsetting Mia who was playing with her teddies there. This resulted in the two of them having a full-blown, fist-flying fight amidst the Lego carnage. Tears and screams of 'Mummeeeeee!' led to me being fully distracted, burning the sausages and left me feeling desperate. I so wanted Katie to think my two children were little angels. Or, at least, spirited and quirky. Not a chance. Rude, maybe. Hard work, definitely.

'Dinner time,' I called out, half-heartedly. Meal times were always a challenge. Sitting together at the table seemed to be the perfect opportunity to argue some more and basically just be nasty to each other. But I needed to get ready.

'Aren't you having any, Mummy?' Mia asked.

'No. I'm meeting a friend, remember?'

'Who is she?' Samuel asked.

'You've never met. It's an old friend from when I was younger. I'm just going to have a quick shower. If I put the TV on, will you eat nicely, please? Katie will be here soon.'

Running upstairs, I felt breathless. The day was monumental. Burnt sausages and bickering children aside, I'd be making love with Robin for the first time that night. I hadn't slept with anyone in years which made me nervous. But this was Robin, and I had already fallen deeply, and profoundly, in love with him. Our relationship was already beautiful, and I could only imagine how a level of intimacy would enhance it. Like when my apple tree erupted into a soft, silky blanket of pink blossom, and it seemed hard to believe that anything could be more wonderful until the sweet fruit burst from within.

Relieved that I shaved my legs the night before, I stood under the steaming hot shower and washed away the burnt sausage smell. I wanted to stand there longer, in the hot water, but time didn't permit, so I got out and wrapped my hair in a towel whilst I dressed. Slightly self-conscious, I pulled on my new, matching, deep-red underwear, tights, and a simple – but flattering – knee-length black dress. I wondered if it was too much and glanced back at my jeans. No. The night was special.

How long did I have left? Twenty minutes? Crap. No time to style my hair, so I roughly blow-dried it before applying my make-up. I really wanted to paint my nails. No time left.

A car pulled up outside. *Katie*. Was I ready? I had to be. Running downstairs, I wondered what mess the children had made. Groaning at the scene, I discovered that Mia had spilt her drink and Samuel's beans had mostly been abandoned off the sides of his plate as he tried to cut his sausages. A stab of guilt: I knew he struggled with a knife and fork.

'Mia, can you clear the table, please?' I asked.

'But we haven't had pudding,' Mia said.

'There's ice-pops in the freezer. Can you sort them?'

The door-bell rang. Katie came in, armed with homework books. I really hoped the children gave her a chance to do some of it. I wasn't overly hopeful – ever the realist. I explained bedtimes and left, after copious bedtime kisses and hugs. Katie looked a bit nervous. More guilt. But I was on my way to Robin and nothing could spoil it.

*

He was in his car, waiting in the hotel carpark. My heart was beating so hard I feared it could be seen through my dress. *Calm down*, I thought, but it was impossible. A sip of my water before reaching for the door handle. Quick mascara check. Good. Not smudged.

Here goes...

Chapter 5

May 2012

I was deep in concentration when Robin called on Skype. I glanced at the clock. Nearly midnight. How did it get that late?

'Hi, love. So sorry; I lost track of time. You OK?' Robin said.

'Yes. I didn't notice the time, anyway.'

'How was Samuel today?'

He always asked about Samuel. It made me happy that he cared.

'Not too bad. He's spending most of his days either sitting in the cloakroom on his own or in the school office doing colouring.'

'That's not exactly ideal,' he said.

'I know. But I don't know what the alternatives are. School have drawn a blank with everything they've tried and exhausted all strategies known to them, so now we just have to wait for the assessment. He hasn't been excluded again, though. Bonus.'

'I suppose it's a small bonus. When's the assessment?'

'I have no idea. It's a long wait, though.'

Robin nodded slowly. 'What are you up to?'

'Researching.'

'What do you mean?'

'I've seen a job advertised. I really want it.'

Robin looked surprised. 'That's brilliant. What's it for?'

'Head of English at a local independent school. The pay's good.'

'What do you need to do?'

'Interview and a presentation on my goals and plans.'

'Do you have a plan?'

'Many!' I said. 'I can make huge changes to the department. I just need the panel at the interview to understand that.'

'Well, don't let me keep you. I'll sit with you on Skype whilst you work,' Robin said.

I had loved being immersed in the world of teaching again and looked forward to walking into my classrooms every day, feeling energised and enthusiastic. This was what I was born to do. The new job would be perfect for me. I craved the extra responsibility it offered. It had my name written all over it, and I would do anything to ensure that I was prepared enough to be the only suitable candidate for the position.

I felt great whilst planning my presentation. Spreadsheets. PowerPoint presentations. Ideas. A five-year plan. A ten-year plan. Every detail had been planned explicitly, and I knew that there was no question that could stump me in the interview as I had written down every possible one with a well thought-out answer and memorised them all. Nothing had been neglected. This job was mine.

*

I got the position. In all honesty, I surprised myself despite my over-confidence and weeks of preparation. The competition was extremely high, and my inexperience suddenly felt like a concern. However, I did it. In September I would start at my new job.

Chapter 6

July 2012

The past few months had been unbearable. According to everyone at his school Samuel was nothing but a rude and naughty boy. I received daily complaints, and Samuel was left in the office most of the day doing colouring whilst talking to the receptionist. He hadn't learnt a thing since he started school, and I was terrified about what damage was being done to his self-esteem and mental health. He already saw himself as a failure, declaring that he couldn't do anything. Staying at this school simply wasn't an option.

After some extensive research and asking around, I found a new school. There was a mixture of excitement and nerves surrounding this action. What if it wasn't as good as it seemed? What if it turned out to be another mistake? Was I going to end up screwing up my children's education completely by doing this?

There was no way to know for sure until we dived in head first and tried it. It would definitely be an improvement for Samuel; of that I had no doubt. It simply couldn't be worse than where he was. However, Mia was anxious and unsure.

'What if I don't make any new friends?'

'But you will. Why wouldn't you? You're funny and friendly. They'll all want to be your friend.'

I knew that Mia would love the school once she saw it, so we planned to visit. Unsure how their current school would react to finding out that I was looking at other schools, I informed the school office that Mia had a doctor's appointment. I only took Mia as I wanted her to have the best possible experience of the new school without the stress of Samuel playing up.

Without feeling any guilt, I dropped Samuel at school and drove Mia to the new school. The Head was there to greet us with a genuine smile and reassuring handshake. I already liked the place.

'Welcome to our school. I'm Mrs Allan, the head teacher. Would you like to come and see around?'

As we walked around the school, the children looked as if they were at home with an air of confidence and contentment. The staff, too, looked positive and welcoming; if the strain of the end of the school year was being felt by them it certainly wasn't obvious to me or the children.

Mia walked around the school in silence. I tried to read her expression, but her feelings were being carefully concealed.

'What do you think?' I whispered.

'It's nice.'

Nice? That's positive, right? I'll take it.

Mrs Allan was near the end of her tour. She opened a door, revealing a new looking dance studio with mirrored walls. She beamed at Mia.

'Do you like dancing?' she asked Mia.

Mia's eyes lit up. 'Yeah, I love it.'

'Well, we have been extremely lucky that the PTA have funded this room for us. During the day it is used as an extra room for small groups or reading, but at lunchtimes we have a Street Dance club and a Junior Strictly club which you could join.'

Mia started jumping up and down and took my hand. 'Mummy, I'm so excited. When can we come back?'

With a sigh of relief, I realised that everything was going to be OK.

Chapter 7

August 2012

The holidays were coming to an end. I thought I would love having six weeks at home with the children, with no responsibilities and a welcome break from the usual stress and routine of term time. So, why did I feel so low?

The year had been mad. There had been daily stress connected with Samuel's school experience and the lack of education he was receiving. I had been on the receiving end of some difficult emotions from Mia who had been talking about her dad quite a lot recently. Trying to manage everything to do with the children, their homework, after-school activities and looking after our home, all on my own, had left me permanently firing on all cylinders during term-time and barely pausing for breath. Oh, and then there was the little additional element that was my first year of full-time teaching in five years. Every day there had been challenge after challenge, which I had thrown all of my energy and emotion into, with a permanent feeling of 'what's next?'

But, as the summer holidays stretched ahead of us, I felt my mood plummeting like I was sinking in a pool of thick, oozy glue. My brain had shut down. There was a heaviness around me, on me, in me, and I couldn't shift it. It made me tired and I felt... What did I feel?

Numb. I felt nothing.

The sound of the children playing was too loud. Too sharp. Too spiky. Inside I was screaming. Outside I showed no emotion. The children didn't notice. Why would they? They shouldn't notice. But I was irritable and snapped at them. I couldn't stop myself. Then I felt the self-loathing and guilt that always followed.

So, we would go out. Into town. To the park. To the forest. Anywhere that would have given me pleasure before. I went searching for it. It felt like there should be signs everywhere, pinned to trees and lampposts, helping me find it. *Lost: Happiness.* Like I was looking for a lost dog. Hoping to find it hiding somewhere; maybe in the spot where we went for picnics last summer?

It wasn't there. It wasn't anywhere. But the black dog found me. He was just hiding. Happiness was still lurking somewhere just a little out of reach.

The world had left me behind. When did it do that? When we were out, I didn't feel connected with anything. Everyone around me was muffled and moving too fast. I wasn't there with them. I could see them all, but they couldn't see me. I wasn't really there.

This wasn't me. I got lost, and I didn't know how to return.

Chapter 8

September 2012

It felt all too familiar. Two pairs of brand-new, polished school shoes stood to attention by the door. Two sets of uniform were ironed and ready to go. And two children excitedly – and nervously – busied themselves around the house getting ready for their first day at their new school.

And yes, I had the same levels of nerves, guilt and nausea that accompanied this same day last year although this time it was worse. Much worse. Because, this year, the odds were higher. Unlike last September I knew that Samuel was unlikely to settle at school. I envied last year's ignorance.

On top of this it was the first day of my new job. And I felt a little sick.

I had requested a late start at work, to enable me to take the children into their classrooms this year. I didn't think I could have stomached dropping them both at breakfast club today. Mia was scared. Really scared. She was such a sensitive little soul, and she gripped my hand tightly. When we got to the Year 1 classroom she hugged me tightly, and I was grateful that I made sure I could be here to do this with her. Resisting the urge to cry, I gently eased her towards the door, and she went in without a fuss.

Just Samuel left. *Oh God, please don't make this too hard, Samuel,* I thought.

Samuel was holding my hand tightly whilst gently rubbing his favourite toy rhino on his face. He was scared. Rhino would hopefully ease his nerves, but I felt my heart breaking. *I can't do this again. What if he cries all day? What if he refuses to go in? What if he walks around the classroom screaming?*

Reading my mind, his teacher held her hand out to Samuel.

'We're going to be fine. Try not to worry,' she said.

And Samuel walked straight into the classroom and sat on the carpet, close to Mia, his face buried in Rhino. He was in. And he wasn't crying.

Unlike me.

Big, fat tears started rolling down my cheeks, and I wiped them away in embarrassment as I hurried out of the school.

Be brave, wonderful children. Braver than me. You've got this.

＊

The day was a success. I managed to get to my school in plenty of time for second period, ready to teach my first class. The class was so much smaller than what I was used to, and I really felt like I could give the children the attention they deserved. I loved every minute of my first day.

I collected Mia and Samuel from the after-school club, a little nervously, expecting the worst. But it was fine. They had a good day. Samuel had managed to cope reasonably well, and it was an overall success. And breathe. The relief was immense.

Driving towards my home, I saw a car parked on the road outside. A silver Audi, shining in the early evening sun. I caught my breath. *No. It can't be.* My heart started to quicken, and I held my breath. *Robin?*

Then I could see him. Grinning, as he recognised my car, he got out to meet me. I gasped.

'Oh my god.'

'What?' Mia asked.

'A friend of mine. He lives a long way away. What on Earth's he doing here?'

I parked in my drive, and Robin was there, opening my door, holding a beautiful arrangement of flowers. Roses and lilies in red, pink and white.

'Hey,' he said, warmly, and leant forwards to kiss me. His soft, warm lips tasted faintly of coffee, and he smelt divine.

'What are you doing here?' I said, pulling him into a hug and burying my face in his neck. 'It's so good to see you.'

He held me tightly but said nothing. I could feel his heart pounding through my breasts and our deep breaths combined in a hot mix of excitement.

Robin squeezed me tightly then let go, grinning at the children as they got out of the car looking confused and startled. I hadn't ever mentioned Robin to them. I thought it would be too confusing as we rarely saw each other.

'You must be Samuel and Mia. It's lovely to meet you both. Hang on a minute, I have something for you.' He paced back to the car, reached inside and came back with two large, soft bears. 'I heard that you've all had a big day. First day in new schools for everyone? Am I right?'

The children nodded and agreed, looking longingly at the bears being hugged into Robin's chest.

'These are for you two. For being brave today.'

Mia and Samuel squealed in excitement and took a bear each, hugging them adoringly.

'You didn't need to do this,' I said, feeling overwhelmed but very happy.

'Yes, I did. It's a big day. Huge, in fact. And I'm taking you all to dinner. Who fancies pizza?'

The children jumped up and down and exclaimed in excitement. The fact that they had no idea who this man was seemed to be irrelevant when soft bears and pizza were on offer. I placed my flowers on the car roof and pulled Robin into my arms again.

'Thank you. This means the world to me.'

'You deserve it.'

And there we stood, immersed in our bubble, as one. This was where I belonged. In his arms. Always.

'How long are you here for?' I whispered into his

ear whilst inhaling the scent from his neck. It was intoxicating.

'I need to go back tomorrow. That's if I can find somewhere to stay tonight.'

I took a deep breath and bit my lip as I squeezed him tightly.

'I'm sure I can find somewhere for you to sleep.'

'Sofa? Floor?'

'Something like that,' I answered.

'Let's get pizza,' Samuel shouted, jumping up and down, unable to contain his excitement.

Robin and I took a step away from each other, and I grinned at Samuel. 'OK. Let's drop off our things in the house and get ready to go.' Robin held my hand as we walked towards the front door, and my heart swelled. We instantly felt like a family. Everything I had ever wanted was right there, in my reach, and I had never felt so happy.

*

The next morning, we all woke up early to get ready for school. The children would be attending breakfast club so that I could get to work. Robin was dressed and tying his shoelaces, sitting on the end of my bed. My room was stuffy and smelt of our combined bodies, making me hungry for more. I needed him. I had a desperate urge to keep him close. The thought of him leaving was tearing up my insides, and I struggled to swallow; a large knot of despair grew steadily in my throat as I felt the magnetic pull of our bodies under threat.

'Can you stay a bit longer?' I asked.

Robin sighed heavily, stood up and walked over to me. He embraced me tightly, one hand stroking my hair, and I felt myself sink comfortably into the contours of his body. This felt natural. Like it was meant to be. We combined together to make a whole and wrenching us apart would leave me empty. Incomplete.

'I'm sorry. I have to go. I have a deadline coming up, and I write best in my office, with all of my stuff to hand.'

'Just one more night? You can use my computer today.' I could hear the desperation in my voice, but I didn't care.

'I'm sorry, love. I can't.' We held each other in silence. 'I can sit with you on Skype later, though?'

It wasn't the same. I wanted to be able to feel the warmth of his body against mine. Smell him. Feel the rise and fall of his heartbeat as I rested my head on his chest.

'OK,' I said. 'That'll be nice.' *Don't leave me. I need you. This is ripping me apart.*

Then he was gone. And a small part of me crumbled.

Chapter 9

October 2012

It took a year to reach the point of Samuel's assessment for autism spectrum disorder. I woke up with a strange feeling in my stomach which I couldn't quite place. Nerves? Why would I feel nervous, though? He was either autistic or he wasn't. It wasn't anything to be scared of. It wasn't going to change our day-to-day life at all by knowing one way or the other. But the feeling didn't go away.

I picked Samuel up from school and headed over to the hospital.

'Why do I need to go to the hospital, Mummy?'

'Because a doctor is going to see if they can do anything to help you at school.'

'What will the doctor do to me?' His eyes were large, and I could see the fear hiding behind them.

'No, that's not what I meant. The doctor isn't

going to do anything to you. The doctor wants to meet you to see if there is anything we can do at school to help you.'

'Not an operation?'

I squeezed his hand. 'No, Sammy. Not an operation. Nothing like that.'

*

We were called into the room by the educational psychologist, and Samuel clung onto me tightly. I felt guilty for putting him through this. I spent so much time feeling guilty these days. The assessment was an interesting experience. I was instructed to stay on a chair in the corner of the room and make no attempt to communicate with Samuel. He was then asked various questions and encouraged to demonstrate his abilities in different activities. Samuel behaved beautifully. To be honest, it wasn't what I was hoping for. I wanted him to scream or hide under the table: anything that would demonstrate the type of behaviour that had become commonplace in the classroom. But no. He answered the questions politely and enjoyed the games and activities so much that he didn't want to leave.

The psychologist smiled towards me at the end of the assessment.

'That's it. All done. There will be a follow-up appointment with the paediatrician, but I don't have any concerns. His imaginative play is a bit limited but it's there. Same goes for eye contact. It isn't consistent, but he does occasionally use it. Developmentally he's a bit behind, but I know that there were issues last year at school. You may find that things start to improve now that he has changed school.'

What did this all mean? Was his behaviour, in fact, a choice by him? Should he be able to control himself better? Why was every day such a struggle for him, then?

'Oh. OK,' I said. *Now what?* 'What do I do now, then?'

'Wait for the paediatrician appointment, but I suggest you just give him time to settle into his new school. The right environment can do wonders for a child's development.'

I left, feeling like my emotions had been through a spin cycle. I knew that I should feel relief: my son didn't have autism. But, instead, I just felt confused and a little lost.

What now?

*

Staring at my phone, I read the email again from the Special Educational Needs Coordinator, Mr Hart. He wanted to meet to discuss how Samuel was settling in. The usual panic rose from deep inside my stomach. I could easily imagine what kind of behaviour was going to be discussed.

Walking into school, I braced myself for the inevitable. I had had this conversation many, many times before. I could do this.

So, why did I feel a little nausea? Would anyone be able to see that my hands were shaking?

I was taken into the Year 1 classroom once it had cleared at the end of the day and was asked to sit down at a table. The chairs were designed for very young children and my knees felt unnaturally high as I sat. It was almost comical. Like a frog: legs bent, ready to bounce far, far away from the foreboding classroom. Any other time this image in my head would have made me laugh. However, the fleeting thought didn't make it as far as the corners of my mouth.

'I was a bit surprised that Samuel was discharged so quickly by the paediatrician following his ASD assessment. Did she give any indication of what happens now?' Mr Hart asked.

'No. I have no idea what I'm supposed to do. If he hasn't got autism, then how am I supposed to know what else is going on?'

'Well, all we can do for now is try and make each day easier. I'm working with his class teacher to implement some new techniques and activities which may help.'

Samuel's behaviour in school deteriorated once he got to know his new class and his inhibitions diminished. His initial fear on his first day, which brought a false hope of calm, was replaced by usual squeals, shouting, interruptions and erratic behaviour. The difference, however, was that this school approached the challenging behaviour using positive strategies and were willing to try and overcome his difficulties with careful support.

I could feel my hands relaxing as the shakiness started to wear off.

'Ultimately, it doesn't really matter here what the concluding diagnosis will be. It won't change the way we address his difficulties. We'll continue to assess where Samuel needs more help and try to find the best way to enable him to get it. We don't need a diagnosis to do that.'

That made sense. Treat the symptoms, not the cause. This was all positive and proactive, and the relief trickled warmly through me.

Chapter 10

November 2012

As if Samuel's problems at school weren't enough for him to deal with, he had other issues thrown in too. Samuel frequently became sick. Every few weeks he would have a raging high temperature, vomit and become floppy and lethargic. I would take him to the doctors every time just to be told that it was viral. 'Take him home and give him paracetamol.' It broke my heart to see him so sick.

Mia learnt to accept Samuel as a sickly child. She was gentle and caring with him. And I would feel growing guilt every time at how Samuel's needs would draw my attention away from Mia.

In the end, I stopped taking him to the doctor when he became sick. It felt cruel: dragging him down to the busy surgery only to be told to go home again. I was also aware that I was wasting their time. So, we stopped going, but the regularity of his sick days continued every few weeks.

*

Samuel was lying in bed with a fever, barely able to stay awake, and I decided that he was sick enough to warrant a trip to the GP. He was hot, vomiting and unable to even drink water. I carried him into the doctor's room, explaining how I was concerned about keeping him hydrated. The GP then did something that nobody had ever done before: he looked in Samuel's mouth.

'It's tonsillitis. I'll write a prescription for antibiotics and he should be better in no time.'

Everything suddenly seemed to click into place. Samuel had suffered from undiagnosed, recurring tonsillitis all his life, and nobody had ever checked. I didn't suspect tonsillitis as he never complained of a sore throat. All this time, his sickness and fever could have been treated.

I felt really angry. For five years, Samuel had suffered. *Five years!* The injustice of it lay heavily within me. Although I knew that I would be able to help him in future. I was an expert at spotting the signs. Next time, I'd be ready.

Chapter 11

February 2013

The revelation that brought knowledge of the cause of Samuel's sickness had been tainted by constant frustration. I could tell when he was getting sick: the pale complexion, the black shadows under his eyes, the red ring around his eyelids, a temperature over forty degrees and extreme lethargy. He complained of a headache and a stomach ache. I knew then that we had twenty-four hours before he was hardly able to stay awake and vomiting.

However, trying to convince a GP that I knew my child, was pointless. I would explain, every time, that Samuel suffered from recurring tonsillitis, and I would be told, every time, that it was viral.

'The white spots just haven't appeared on his tonsils yet. He's always like this at first but then the spots appear,' I would say each time I took him to the surgery.

'Then, wait until the white spots appear and bring him back.'

'But he will be really sick by then. It knocks him out, and he can't even walk. If he starts the antibiotics now he won't get to that stage.'

It never worked. I always had to carry him back into the surgery, twelve hours later, to get the prescription. I understood that they were told not to overprescribe antibiotics, but it was so frustrating when I knew every time that Samuel needed them and would not start to recover without them. Without treatment, the bacteria stayed within his system for a couple of weeks, making recovery difficult. Then, within the next few weeks, he would get sick again. He needed the antibiotics.

Some mornings he would wake complaining of a headache. The usual panic came crashing down on me as I prepared to go to work and dreaded phoning in sick *again*. So, I would dose him up with paracetamol and send him into school, consumed with guilt, and waited for the phone call, wondering if – for once – maybe I had got it wrong. Maybe it was just a headache. Maybe he would be OK.

He never was. Every time I would receive a phone call some time mid-afternoon, and I would arrive at school to find Samuel asleep on the classroom floor. And I would fight the tears as I lifted his limp body into my arms, trying unsuccessfully to suppress the raging guilt which burned in the pit of my stomach.

I would drive straight to the GP surgery and carry him in, hoping that the white spots were evident. Sometimes they were, and I would want to punch the air with relief as a prescription was handed over to me. But, I was usually sent away to wait. It felt so unfair. I knew what Samuel needed. I always knew. Not once had I been wrong. Yet my instincts meant nothing.

Chapter 12

May 2013

A heatwave hit us out of nowhere. We were all feeling uncomfortable, and Mia was sitting in the paddling pool in the garden. Samuel came and sat on my lap.

'My tummy hurts,' he said.

Here we go again.

'OK. Do you just want to stay here and have a cuddle?'

He nodded and rested his head on my shoulder, closing his eyes. I felt his forehead. It was hot to touch.

'Will I need the magic medicine, Mummy?'

I sighed. 'I think you probably will. Just rest for now.'

After a couple of hours, I looked inside his mouth. 'There aren't any white spots yet. Do you want to have a little sleep? I think we'll end up going to the doctors tonight.'

He agreed, and I carried him up to my bed. He was asleep in minutes. Quietly, I crept out and joined Mia in the garden.

'Is Samuel sick again?' Mia asked.

'Yes. We'll probably have to take him to see the doctor later.'

'What about tea?' Mia asked. I smiled. It was such a simple life when all you had to worry about was where your next meal was coming from.

'Don't you worry about that. I'll feed you somehow.'

*

It was five o'clock when Samuel woke, crying gently. On examining his throat, I could see white patches covering both tonsils.

'Come on then. Time to go,' I said. 'Mia, can you get ready to leave, please?'

I hurriedly got both children into the car and drove to the out-of-hours surgery at the hospital. The car park was busy, and I reluctantly parked further from the entrance, knowing that I would need to carry Samuel all the way. The sun was beating down on us unforgivably, making the effort of lifting Samuel more extreme and uncomfortable.

Samuel's skin against mine was alarmingly warm, and I struggled with him into a crowded waiting area.

'It's about a two-hour wait,' the receptionist said.

'There aren't any chairs,' I answered, feeling my back and knees straining under the weight of Samuel.

'Sorry, we're busy.'

I gently laid Samuel down by the open door, so he could get a draft onto his feverish body, and we waited. Mia played just outside the door; she was twirling around, watching her summer dress floating airily in the breeze. Samuel slept for about an hour. Doctors walked past his sleeping body, not paying him any attention. What if he was seriously sick? Would anybody care?

Samuel woke up and started crying quietly. I pulled him onto my lap feeling more and more cross with our situation.

'I'm going to be sick,' he said.

Looking around desperately, I noticed a pile of sick bowls near the reception. Levering Samuel back onto the floor, I dashed over to collect one for him – just in time – although some vomit ended up on his clothes. I expected someone to come and help. A doctor, nurse, receptionist… anybody. Nobody moved. I could feel the threat of tears burning behind my eyes as I pleaded internally for someone to help us.

Another patient came over and rested her hand on my shoulder. 'Can I help at all?' she asked. I wanted to hug her, but I was holding a bowl of vomit.

'I don't know. I don't know what to do,' I said.

'I have some baby wipes. I can help you clean him up.'

The relief of having somebody there to help was immense. A stranger, who had no need to help, was mopping up vomit off my child whilst the receptionist pretended not to notice.

Resting Samuel back down on the ground, where

he promptly lay back down to sleep again, I approached the receptionist, vomit bowl in my hand.

'My son has been sick.' *As if you haven't noticed.* 'What should I do with this?'

'There's a bin in the toilets.'

'And where are they?'

'I'll let you through this door, and they're along the corridor.'

She buzzed me through the door, and I looked up and down the deserted corridor. Where was everybody? Eventually, I found a toilet and entered, looking for an appropriate bin for a vomit bowl. There was just a bin for paper towels. *That can't be right. Where's the bin for human waste? Shouldn't there be yellow bags for this?*

A cleaner walked in. 'Where should I put this, please?'

She gestured to the bin and spoke in a different language.

'But it's been sick in. Should it really go in here?' *Uncovered, for everyone to see?*

She pointed again, more determinedly this time, and I placed it in there with a sigh of frustration. This didn't seem right, but I wanted to get back to Samuel and Mia. I threw it in the bin, washed my hands and left.

It took almost two hours to be seen by a nurse. During those two hours medical staff had arrived or left for their shifts and walked straight past Samuel's sleeping body on the floor. Nobody checked on him. Nobody offered water or a more appropriate place for him to lie down to wait. It made me think of how an overstretched hospital in a disadvantaged country must operate. Not an NHS out-of-hours department.

Antibiotics were prescribed, and I wondered with desperation how many more times we would have to go through this.

Chapter 13

February 2014

I knew that things would change after Samuel's tonsillectomy. I had waited in desperation for things to change. Expecting nothing but a positive outcome, I didn't feel prepared for what happened next. For the first time in seven years, Samuel was well.

Gone was the slightly grey complexion and black shadows around his eyes. Gone was the daily fatigue and collapsing into bed by six o'clock every evening. Gone were the quiet moments of exhausted and slightly sickly cuddles.

Samuel was feeling better.

Of course, I was delighted. I shuddered to think just how unwell Samuel must have felt for his whole life, never completely free of infection in his tonsils. It must have made him so tired every day even when I assumed that he was feeling better. He couldn't have been because this was what feeling better was like.

And our lives were suddenly turned upside down.

The level of Samuel's energy was startling. He woke up early every day and was instantly wide awake. More than wide awake: he was hyperactive. Samuel charged around the house, screaming and shouting, throwing things, starting activities then discarding them moments later and creating a trail of mess and destruction in his wake.

He had a slightly drunk demeanour and look in his eyes; they darted around the room taking in everything but settling on nothing. I tried to hold him, to calm him down, but he screamed and wriggled free, refusing to listen to anything I had to say.

We had no more conversations, but he would shout at me. He pushed me, scratched me, threw things at me and damaged his own toys and items within the house. He was out of control.

Night-time had become unbearable. Samuel didn't know how to sleep. He had no idea how to physically and mentally wind himself down enough to enable him to sleep. It had been three weeks since his operation and every night was the same. The hyperactivity that dominated our days collided full force with bedtime leaving us in a whirlwind of activity and negativity. Kicking a football around the house at ten o'clock at night became the norm.

It felt like we were at crisis point. I didn't know what to do. I was sure that Samuel was lost somewhere inside the tornado, but I just couldn't find him. Our life became our little secret: an inferno behind closed doors. To everybody else it was the same as it had always been, but inside I was breaking.

Alone. Overwhelmed. Trying to contain and control Samuel's behaviour was all consuming and had taken over my life. I didn't phone any of my friends anymore. Nobody came to visit. I didn't dare leave the house except for school. I had completely isolated myself in our fragile little bubble.

The only person who had even a tiny understanding of how things had escalated in my fractured world was Robin. He would phone every day and come online at night, once the house was calm and still, and allow me to vent towards him. He always listened. And he tried to offer advice and support. For this, I was grateful. But I also felt angry and let down. Why wouldn't he come and help me in my time of need? Why had he not suggested coming over one evening to give me something to look forward to? It would be a welcome and much needed distraction: a way to release the simmering ball of pain which nestled so easily in my chest.

I don't know what to do.

Chapter 14

April 2014

The initial shock of Samuel's behaviour started to wear off, leaving me just a tiny bit of headspace to think about what had happened. Samuel's behaviours had spiralled out of control. I could only wish for the days when his focus and emotional development were just a complication for school and not home. His behaviours and reactions to everyday situations had started to monopolise my family's every move, every day.

School had become extremely difficult. Samuel's inability to cope within the classroom was affecting his education. He was struggling to concentrate for longer than a few minutes, he couldn't sit still and was reacting alarmingly to sensory stimulation. The lights, the sounds and the smells of the school environment were a massive distraction.

After school and weekends were almost unbearable. We couldn't go out in public without risking overwhelming meltdowns which I was only just learning how to react to. I certainly couldn't control them. He screamed in the car and threw things at me whilst I was driving. He hit me and Mia. She was fed up with it. I didn't know how to explain it all to Mia to help her understand. How could I when I didn't understand?

In the aftermath of a particularly difficult evening, when Samuel had refused to go to bed and had thrown things at me, I sat on the sofa and cried. I seemed to cry every night at bedtime. It was too hard. I was constantly walking on egg shells and putting out fires, and it was mentally and physically exhausting. That evening, however, I received a text as I cried from Robin.

How are you doing? xx

Such an innocent question. Such an overwhelming answer.

Not great, I replied.

Give me five minutes… he wrote. Relief. Having someone to share this draining experience with was just what I needed.

We talked and talked for hours. It was good to have someone just to vent to, and who listened wholly and compassionately. Nobody knew how hard things had become, and it suddenly felt like I had everything to unload.

'I've been doing a bit of reading up online,' he said. 'What do you know about ADHD?'

I hesitated. It had crossed my mind many times but quickly been dismissed. Attention Deficit Hyperactivity Disorder was one of the most unrecognised conditions that I knew of. During my time working in schools, I had heard too many negative and insulting comments about children with the condition.

Before I had my own children, a teacher had once warned me that a child I was about to teach had not had his Ritalin that day, and he was likely to be 'a nightmare'. He had ended up becoming so disruptive that he was physically escorted from the room by two members of staff against his will. I remember inwardly blaming the parent. I wasn't sure what I was blaming the parent for. Lack of discipline? Too many sweets? Artificial sweeteners? Or just neglecting to drug her child that day? To my shame, it was a negative experience in my memory.

I was completely ashamed of the way I had judged hyperactive children and their parents before. I was naïve and ignorant. Becoming a parent had brought a new level of understanding, especially with Samuel around. However, people often aren't understanding when it comes to other people's children. People don't learn the facts of various conditions. Why should they if it doesn't concern them? People can be ignorant. I once read a newspaper report suggesting that benefits to parents of children with ADHD should be cut. It referred to the condition as *naughty child syndrome* and said that parents were being rewarded for bad parenting. This sickened me to my core. The journalist was describing me and Samuel. That's what people would think.

To have a diagnosis of ADHD felt like a parenting fail. That's how people would react to it. And I didn't think I was a bad parent. I tried not to be. Who's to judge this, though? Maybe I was. Maybe I was getting everything wrong. Either way, I didn't think I wanted my child to be labelled with ADHD.

Robin's words, however, didn't echo my concerns.

'He has all of the symptoms. I would even say that I think he has quite a severe case of ADHD. You can't carry on like this. Sweetie, you need help,' he said.

I knew that he was right. We needed help. We needed to see the GP.

Chapter 15

May 2014

After reading up on countless websites concerning ADHD, and conditions that could present themselves as ADHD but be something entirely different, I armed myself with a folder full of print-outs of symptoms (highlighted and underlined in a bid to reassure myself when confronted by a sceptical doctor) and walked into the GP surgery.

I was expecting a fight, and I was ready for one. Everything so far with Samuel, from appointments about his development to appealing for a tonsillectomy, had been a battle. Nothing was ever easy. Why should this have been any different?

Samuel wasn't keen about going.

'But why do I need to see a doctor? I'm not poorly.'

'I know you're not, but the doctor may have some ideas about why you struggle to concentrate. We can ask him for help with that.'

'Will he need to do an operation?' he asked. I pulled him into my arms and kissed the top of his head, breathing in the scent of his shampoo and feeling overwhelming guilt for putting him through this.

'No, Sammy. Like you said, you're not poorly. Nobody is going to operate on you.'

In the waiting room, Samuel looked nervous. I could relate: my heart was pounding as I gripped tightly to the folder of evidence on my lap. How would I start this conversation with the GP? *I was reading on the internet and I am wondering if my son has ADHD…* In my head it sounded like something an overly neurotic mother would say.

'Samuel May to room eight, please.'

Here we go, I thought, taking Samuel's hand, and we nervously approached the door. The GP was somebody I hadn't seen before, but his smile was confident and welcoming as he showed us inside. The room felt clinical, and I could sense Samuel's panic beside me. I reached for his hand.

'Samuel's been really struggling at school. Well, at home too. Everywhere, really…' and it all came flooding out of me in torrential waves. And it felt good. Our dirty secret, which had been kept hidden so precariously behind closed doors, was being released to the world. Suddenly, it wasn't just me. Somebody who had the power to help was sat opposite me, listening.

And he really listened. He didn't just give the impression that he gave a damn for the duration of the ten-minute appointment, and then it would all be over. He let me talk, and he didn't move or interrupt until I paused for breath.

Samuel had abandoned his chair next to me and was exploring around the room whilst I talked. I didn't take any notice: I was used to his constant activity. When I came to a natural break in my woeful monologue, I studied the doctor's face for a clue to show me what he was thinking. His brow was furrowed as he leant towards me in his chair.

'I think that they were right to not rush into an autism diagnosis. I don't think he has autism. However, from what you have said, and going by the fact that Samuel has touched everything within his reach in this room since you entered, I suggest we consider ADHD as a real possibility. I will need to refer Samuel to CAMHS for assessment. Are you happy for me to do this?'

I hadn't even needed to open the folder of evidence which was getting sweaty and uncomfortable in my tight grip. There was no fight. He listened. And he believed me.

There was nothing left to do but wait.

Chapter 16

June 2014

The wait for a CAMHS appointment seemed endless. Knowing that we had at least started the long journey to get Samuel any help that may be available felt like progress, but we had a long way to go. And, in the meantime, Samuel continued to struggle which affected his behaviour and reactions to everyday situations all the time. This was tough: for him, his teachers, me, his sister and anybody who had any amount of contact with him.

On a basic level, he struggled to concentrate. When somebody was talking to him he tried to listen, but he was also looking at the bird out of the window, listening to the rhythm the ticking clock was making, wondering what that smell was, trying to ignore the feel of the label in the back of his top and reciting his five-times-table in his head. Then it became hard to listen. Then people got cross with him. It wasn't fair.

He also badly needed routine and any sudden

changes to that were hard for him to accept. A new teacher, a different bedtime, an unexpected evening trip out: these were just a few of the things he struggled with in his routine.

When things seemed to be a bit overwhelming to Samuel, he couldn't think things through or process them properly. Then the emotions started building up and the world seemed like too complicated a place to be in. He went into a shutdown where he wouldn't hear or respond to anything that was said to him. This was a cue to those who knew Samuel to expect a meltdown shortly afterwards. If he was dragged out of his shutdown and made to respond then a meltdown came quicker.

A meltdown is not a tantrum. A child having a tantrum uses it to get what they want when they are angry or frustrated. It can be controlled and stopped by the child when they choose to. A child having a meltdown loses all that control. It is a reaction to too much stimulation, too much stress, too much emotion and not being able to process it and emotionally cope. During a meltdown Samuel would scream, cry, hit himself, hit anything around him and throw his limbs around. He couldn't stop, couldn't remember why he was doing it, couldn't listen to anyone trying to calm him down and couldn't control himself. He didn't care who saw him like that, wasn't embarrassed and didn't know how to stop.

*

I was waiting to collect Samuel outside the main door of the school following an after-school football session. One by one the children filed out to find their parents. Samuel was nowhere to be seen. I approached the coach.

'Hi, is Samuel coming?'

'Who knows? You'll probably need to get him. He's refusing to leave the hall.'

'Has something happened?'

'Yeah, well, he wouldn't join in today. He just went off, running around the school. I can't follow him, you know, when I have all the other kids to watch.'

'No. Of course not.'

I hurried past him and into the school. When I reached the hall, I saw Samuel silently pacing up and down.

'Hey, Sammy. Shall we go?' My voice was quiet, and I tried to make him realise that I wasn't cross with him. Samuel didn't respond.

'Samuel? Shall we go?'

Nothing.

Then, out of nowhere, Samuel bolted out of the hall and towards the front door to the school. In pursuit, I chased him, just in time to see Samuel push past the other parents at the door. *Someone, please stop him,* I thought. Nobody did. They just watched as Samuel ran past them and towards the road. *Shit.*

People parted as I approached the door, and I just got to Samuel as he reached the road. I wrapped my arms around him, but he fought against me, kicking and hitting. He dug his nails into the skin on my hands, drawing blood, but I held tight. Mia came running up behind me.

'He's hurting you, Mummy,' she said.

'It's OK, Mia. It doesn't hurt. Can you go back up to school, sweetie?' I tried to sound calm and in control despite feeling anything but that.

'I don't want to,' Mia said, looking hurt.

'Please, Mia. I need to help Samuel now.'

She walked off, leaving a pang of guilt in my heart knowing that, yet again, Samuel's needs came first.

Summoning up all my strength, and trying not to react to the painful kicks to my shins, I lifted Samuel up and carried him towards the school. Tears were now flowing freely down his face, and he was screaming. Luckily, the front door was still open, and I carried Samuel through the small crowd of parents and into the reception area. There I sat on the floor, wrapping my arms around his writhing body and held him tightly.

For half an hour, Samuel sobbed. Gradually, his fighting eased, leaving him looking vulnerable and broken in my arms. One of the teachers came and spoke to me quietly.

'What can I do?' she asked.

'Do you know if there's a blanket anywhere?'

'I'll get one.'

She left and returned a minute later with a large blanket. Samuel's eyes were tightly closed, and his face was now buried in my chest. The teacher helped to wrap the blanket around us both, and there we sat, not moving, until Samuel drifted off to sleep. I struggled to stand up, still holding Samuel, and carried him to the car. He stirred as I moved him but soon fell back asleep once in the car. I turned to Mia and hugged her, feeling tears well up.

'Come on, sweetie. Let's go home.'

*

I found it hard knowing how to deal with those meltdowns. Thankfully, they weren't too often but did have an enormous impact on the family when he had them. I learnt to move him to a safe and quiet space, hold him tightly against me and not speak. I would hold my hands over his ears, so he wasn't stressed more by sounds and people speaking to him. And we would wait. It could take an hour for him to calm down. Afterwards he sometimes slept, he would become thirsty and could be too exhausted to walk.

Mia got very distressed when she saw this behaviour. She wasn't scared for her own safety when Samuel hit out and threw things, but she was worried that he would hurt himself. Sometimes it made her cry, but often she bottled it up deep inside her. I didn't know if she was afraid or embarrassed to react, or whether she didn't want to add to my trauma. I could see her pain, though. I wished I could take it away. I wished she never had to experience this. I wished none of us did. But it wasn't Samuel's fault: of that I couldn't be surer.

It took a day, for him and me, to recover from these meltdowns. It was draining, upsetting and emotional. I wished that I could find a way to help him better through these situations. But I could only be there and hope that we coped the best that we could.

Chapter 17

July 2014

It was that time of day. The time I dreaded every single day. It could go well, or it could go on for hours and leave me rocking in a corner. It was bedtime. Bedtimes never used to fill me with such dread. We had great routines and early nights, and I would sit smugly every evening knowing that my children were in bed and would stay there all night.

Not any longer.

Mia still went to bed in the way she always had. No arguments, no fights and no tears. I am not sure why it had always been relatively painless with her, but I was very grateful. Samuel was the same until he had his tonsils removed. But afterwards things changed. My bubbly little tornado, who once slept well at night, suddenly became incapable of falling asleep. It would make him upset and frustrated as he told me he just didn't know how to anymore. His brain started going into overdrive every time he lay his head on the pillow and sleep just wouldn't come.

I tried everything: extra stories, different night-lights, singing, leaving him in bed with books to read, CDs of classical music, sitting on his bed with him, sitting on his floor, sitting outside his room, weighted pressure on top of him, rewards and no screens before bedtime. During those early weeks, nothing seemed to work and none of us seemed to get any sleep.

'Samuel, it's really late. You need to get in your bed.'

'No. Never. I'm never going to bed, and you can't make me.'

'I can make you,' I lied.

'No, you can't. You can't make me.'

I knew he was right. I had lost all control of him.

'If you go to bed now, I'll take you to the park after school tomorrow.'

Bribery. What amazing parenting. I tried to ignore the voice inside me, labelling me as a failed mother.

'I don't want to go to the park.'

'OK. If you don't go to bed now, you won't have any cake after your dinner tomorrow.'

'Don't want cake.' He did, however, move closer to the room which he shared with Mia. Mia was lying in bed with headphones on, listening to a Disney Princess album. Poor Mia. Her sleep was really suffering.

'I don't know how to sleep. I'm going to stay awake all night.'

Maybe I needed to change my approach to the situation.

'You don't have to sleep.'

'What?'

'You can stay awake all night, but you need to stay in your bed.'

'I'm staying up all night, I'm staying up all night,' he sang, jumping onto his bed.

'I'm tired, Samuel. So, I'm going to bed. You can stay awake all night, as long as you're in your bed.'

Samuel cheered and bounced up and down on his bed. I kissed Mia and told her to try and sleep with her headphones on. She was too tired to complain.

'Night, then,' I said. Samuel's shouting had suddenly stopped, and he was talking quietly to himself. I could hear him playing with his soft toys, but he was calmer now that he didn't need to fight. After about thirty minutes, I didn't hear any more noises from his room and assumed that he must have fallen asleep.

Was it a parenting win? He was asleep, so maybe. It felt like a win, but I was too exhausted to analyse it in too much detail.

The following nights were unpredictable. Some evenings I managed to get him into his bed using similar tactics, other nights nothing seemed to work. Then, one night, Samuel was thrashing around on his bed, and I started slowly laying some of his bigger soft toys on top of him. Samuel stopped moving. The weight of the toys seemed to calm him, so I put more and more on top. Relatively quickly he fell asleep. It was working!

I read everything I could find on the benefits of weight on children with sensory needs. Everything seemed to back up what I had discovered by accident. And there was more. Children reacted positively with different textures, music and lights. There was so much I could try. Suddenly, I felt just a tiny shred of hope, even when the weight of the teddies seemed to stop working at night.

The next thing I tried, combined with the pile of teddies, was a colour changing bubble lamp in his room. The water made patterns on his ceiling which he watched until he drifted off. I felt victorious. However, it only lasted a few more nights and then the sleepless nights returned.

'I don't know *how* to fall asleep, Mummy,' he said, whilst he practised his forward-rolls across the floor.

I was exhausted. I literally had nothing left to give.

'You need to try, Sammy. Please, try.'

'But I can't. Nothing works.'

After months of trial and error, we seemed to discover a system that worked. Every night he would be read two stories, we'd sing four songs and then he would lie down in bed for a hug. Teddies were piled on him, the bubble lamp went on in the corner of the room, gentle piano music was streamed on my phone next to his bed and he would hold a fibre-optic, colour-changing light which he stroked and watched the lights darting about. I had to sit just in the doorway until he fell asleep. I knew that if I moved he would be up and playing again.

Sometimes it didn't work. Sometimes he was still wide awake and bouncing off the walls hours later. But sometimes was certainly better than all the time. And the nights when it worked made the effort worthwhile.

Chapter 18

August 2014

For the first time in months, I was excitedly anticipating a night out without children. Going out used to be a weekly occurrence. I owned specific clothes just for those nights and would spend hours preparing. Then, after Ben's death, nights out just didn't happen. However, after what had felt like an eternity of waiting, I was seeing Robin again.

Robin had driven across the country and was waiting for me in the pub around the corner. I had asked him not to come straight to the house. Samuel would never sleep if he knew that Robin was there as they had developed a beautiful friendship in the few times they had met. So, I would text Robin when the children were asleep, and he would collect me. After a night out, he would be coming home and spending the night. I was ridiculously excited.

However, I was beginning to think it was a stress that wasn't worth it. Bedtimes were difficult and trying to rush them was counterproductive. Leaving Samuel made me feel nervous, but Annie's daughter Katie was free to babysit, so I took the plunge. I arranged with Katie that I would text once I was ready, so she wouldn't arrive until Samuel was sleeping.

Bedtime was dragging.

'Just one more story,' Samuel asked. 'Please?'

'OK, but this is the last. And then you have to promise me that you'll go to sleep.'

'I promise.'

He was bouncing up and down on the bed and didn't look in the slightest bit sleepy. Damn. As I finished the second story, I started the usual routine of piling teddies on top of him.

'Can you make the teddies tickle me?'

'No.'

'Please? Or talk to me? Can you make them talk to me? I'll go to sleep then.'

Silently groaning, I started a quick conversation between a rhino and a dog whilst nervously glancing at the clock. Mia was waiting patiently in her bed for a goodnight hug.

'That's enough now, Samuel. Sleep time.'

'Can you just...'

'No,' I said, very firmly. And, unbelievably, Samuel lay back and allowed me to prepare him and his nest for sleep.

They were eventually both asleep by eight o'clock. I then had five minutes to get ready. Five! And this involved picking an outfit.

Did I own anything that could be worn on a night out? Of course not. Except for that one top that I never threw out. The top I bought when I lived in London. The top that was – no, surely not – fourteen years old? I think it came back into fashion. That was my story, and I was sticking to it.

Leaving the house was a mission in itself. One last check on the children. Oh, but what if Samuel's music finished and he woke up? I dashed back into the bedroom to restart the music. What if they got thirsty and went downstairs to get water, and I wasn't there? I went back into the bedroom with bottles of water.

Opening a few kitchen cupboards hurriedly, I realised that I had no snacks in the house for Katie. I dashed to the shop opposite to buy chocolates. Then, a quick clean of the toilet due to Samuel spraying everywhere but in the toilet bowl. Nice. Another quick check on the sleeping children. Still sleeping. But then…

What was that? The *doorbell?* I knew it wasn't Katie: I had asked her to text me when she arrived rather than ring the bell. It rang loudly again just as I was throwing myself down the stairs as fast as I could to stop the offenders doing it any more. I opened the door as quietly as I could.

'Hello there, how are you this evening? Oh, are you OK?' she asked, noticing my expression. I must have looked like I was up for a fight. I could feel the panic rising in me, unsure if the children had woken up and wondering who would dare to ring a doorbell during usual children's bedtimes. The lady at the door was collecting money for a charity. She was just doing her job. She certainly didn't deserve to be greeted by a fire-breathing dragon when I opened the door.

'No, I'm not OK,' I whispered, through clenched

teeth. 'My children have just fallen asleep. Why did you ring the doorbell?'

'I'm sorry. I… didn't know.'

'It took me an hour to get them both to bed. Do you fancy donating an hour to get them back to sleep?'

It wasn't fair of me. I knew that. But why would she *do* that? It could have jeopardised my whole night out. Of course there was no way that she would know that.

'I'm sorry. I just didn't know,' she said. She genuinely looked sorry. I felt like a such a cow.

'No, I'm sorry. It's just not easy getting them both to go to sleep.'

'I really hope they haven't woken,' she said, backing away from the door.

'Thanks,' I muttered. *Not as much as I'm hoping,* I thought.

I crept upstairs. Miraculously, they were still asleep. Thank God. Time to put a bit of lippy on, then. *Where's my lippy?* I wondered, searching through all my drawers and pockets. I knew I owned some. I had worn it at Christmas. So, where was it? I found it lurking at the bottom of an old handbag, buried in screwed-up receipts and chewing-gum wrappers. Lipstick on. Just in time as Katie pulled up outside.

Time to leave. Easy, right? Just leave. But, no. Where were my spare keys? God knows; I didn't usually need them. *Fine, I'll leave without keys*, I thought. Money. *How much for a night out? How much is a drink these days?* I had no idea but grabbed a couple of notes and headed for the door. I stopped, feeling uneasy, and then ran back for another check on the children. *Now, really, time to go!*

Robin was waiting patiently in my drive, understanding that knocking on the door could be catastrophic. The first sight of him was magical. His sparkling eyes, delicious smell and wonky smile felt like a drug to me, and I pulled him close. We kissed hungrily.

'Hey,' he said, as we melted away from each other's lips. 'You OK?'

'Perfect,' I whispered. 'It's so good to see you.'

'I know, right? I've been like an excited puppy waiting for this moment.' He put a hand on the back of my head and gently pulled me closer, so I was resting on his neck.

'You smell so good,' he said.

'So do you. I think I'm addicted to your smell.'

A deep sigh from both of us.

'Shall we go? The restaurant said we wouldn't need to book, so we can go straight over there now,' Robin said.

'OK,' I said, reluctantly pulling away from his embrace and taking his warm hand instead as we walked down the road together. This felt right. This was how I was meant to be.

*

The meal tasted good, but I wasn't hungry. All my attention was on the gorgeous man sitting across the table from me, holding one of my hands whilst we ate. It was difficult to eat with just one hand, and the fish spent too much time being reluctantly pushed around my plate, so I gave in trying.

'How was Samuel today?' he asked.

'Oh, you know, much the same as ever. Although I

won the bedtime battle, so I'm feeling victorious now.'

'You're so good with them both. They're lucky to have you as their mum.' He was looking deeply into my eyes and stroking my hands with his thumbs. My heart quivered.

'I've really been missing you,' I said. 'So much. I wish we could see each other more often.'

There was a moment's silence, and Robin stared at my hands whilst he stroked them.

'I know. I feel the same, but it's so difficult. Work feels really pressured these days, and then there's Emily at the weekends. I can't bring her over here. She has dancing on Saturdays, and it wouldn't be fair to drive her across the country with me. And you couldn't drive over to me with the twins, either. It's too far.'

I couldn't answer, overcome with grief. How could he love me and not want to be with me? It didn't make sense. If he truly loved me we would make it work.

Robin kissed my hand and sighed. 'I would love nothing more than to spend all my time with you, but it's not easy. It's like… I feel like this is all I can offer at the moment. I know it isn't fair. It's not enough.'

Another moment's silence. I swallowed, trying to ease the lump in my throat, and battled half-heartedly to keep the tears away.

'I'm so sorry. You deserve so much more,' he said.

'It's not about what I deserve. I love you, and I want to spend more time with you. I need to spend more time with you. Some nights I feel heartbroken sitting alone again, wishing I was in your arms. It's just really hard.'

Robin winced and looked away.

'I could come to you during the school holidays?' I said.

'I have Emily during the holidays. There wouldn't really be room for five of us.'

'I could move closer?'

'But the twins are settled at school. You can't move them again. And Samuel has good support there now.'

'I just miss you.'

'I know. I'm sorry,' he said, looking back into my eyes and squeezing my hands. 'I want to give you more, and I will. I could spend the odd weeknight with you. I just need to get past this deadline. Bear with me?'

I nodded and tried to smile. For Robin, I would wait for an eternity. My heart belonged to him.

Chapter 19

September 2014

It had been the worst day. I was sitting on the stairs, taking deep breaths and hoping that this was it. Hoping it was over. I had nothing left to give. It had started that morning as soon as Samuel woke up. He was hyper and shrieking as he ran around the house. We were late for school after not managing to get him organised in time, and I felt enormous relief as I drove away from their school and towards the sanctuary of work. Mornings were exhausting.

The day didn't improve, and it had been another difficult transition out of school. Samuel had refused to get in the car and had run back through the school and into the playground. Nobody could get near him as he just ran away when anyone started to approach. So, I had followed him around the grounds, with the cheerful site supervisor for company, until Samuel chose his moment to be ready to leave. The school was deserted by that time, and I felt frustrated that this was a normal occurrence for us. Nobody else was still trying to get their children to leave school an hour after classes ended.

As Mia and Samuel got into the car, I assessed the situation. Samuel was now calm. I really needed to buy some milk, but shopping with the children was always difficult. The thought of facing the evening without a cup of tea, however, was enough to give me the strength to drive towards the supermarket.

Exhausted and emotionally drained, I walked down the milk aisle in Sainsbury's clutching Mia's hand. Samuel was spinning, arms outstretched and squealing loudly. A little tornado, releasing energy in the only way he knew how.

I knew it was coming. In fact, I was looking around at all the shoppers I passed, quickly glancing at their faces to see if I had got away with it or not. I knew what they were all thinking as Samuel span noisily past them.

There it was. On the face of that man. He caught my eye, with a disapproving raise of an eyebrow, then leant towards his wife to say something. Maybe it was just a question about which cheese to buy? I didn't think so, though.

I reached for Samuel's shoulders, slowing the spinning down.

'Can you get the milk for me, please?' I asked him.

'Yes, Mummy,' and he ran over to the milk, knocking somebody's trolley to the side.

'Sorry,' I said to the lady, who was pulling her trolley back towards her. She smiled, but it was forced. A fake smile which never reached her eyes. I tried to smile back and took Samuel's hand again.

'Thanks, sweetie. Come on.'

Glancing up, I saw The Look everywhere. On every face around us. My heart pounding, I quickly led both children towards the checkout and away from judging eyes.

Did they know the day I'd had? The week I'd had? The month? They could obviously all do it better than me. It was in their eyes. They knew that they could. If it was them, out shopping with their children, they would all be smiling and humming a merry tune whilst the children helped tick the items on the shopping list off. They certainly wouldn't be doing what Samuel was doing, who had resumed his spinning once we got into the queue to pay.

Did they know that if I gave Samuel the discipline that they probably thought he deserved, it would not calm him down and dampen his spirits? Instead, it would turn the situation into a much louder and more uncontrollable one. Did they see the tears in my eyes and the feeling of desperation because I had run out of ideas?

Did they realise that I was just relieved that we had progressed from screaming? Could they see the bruises on my shins where Samuel had kicked me repeatedly the day before, as I had tried to get him away from school and to the privacy of our home where fewer people could stare?

Did they realise that I had battled this every day whilst also trying to meet the emotional needs of Mia, too? Or, did they just see a mum who couldn't control her child as well as they would be able to? If only they knew.

*

Once I got home, the battles continued. Everything was hard work. In a haze of depression, I willed the day away, as every word and action from my children rolled into one big mess of emotional negativity. My heart felt like it had sunk into the base of my ribcage. My shoulders and head felt heavy. My eyes stung. I didn't know how to shake myself out of it. Some days I lived life to the fullest and loved being alive. Other days, I didn't. Simple as that.

The usual bedtime routine started off well. Samuel had a glass of warm milk and then brushed his teeth. It was whilst I was reading him a story that I realised that it wasn't going to be a smooth bedtime. Samuel bounced up and down next to me on the bed, distracted and agitated.

I turned the different sensory lights on and streamed the gentle piano music through my phone. I tried to tuck him in, but his words had started to turn into grunts accompanied by legs kicking everywhere and teddies thrown around the room. It was at this point that I knew there was no way back. We had reached the end of the line and the only possible outcome was *not* going to bed.

I had no idea of how to proceed. Which was the best way to get through this situation? I just didn't know. I left the room, turning my back on Samuel shouting and throwing toys around. The easiest thing to do would be to leave him to calm down, but that wasn't possible as Mia needed to go to bed. For thirty minutes, Samuel jumped on his bed, shouted and threw Lego out of the door and onto the hall floor. I observed from a distance: not engaging with his behaviour which I feared would fuel the fire. Mia hovered nearby.

'I'm tired, Mummy,' Mia said. I sighed.

'I know, sweetie. I'm sorry. Just give me a minute.'

I walked up the stairs and went to sit on Samuel's bed. 'This has to stop now, Samuel. It's time to sleep.'

'I'm not sleeping.'

'Why not?'

'No. I'm not sleeping.'

'But why?'

'You can't make me, you weirdo.'

A stab of pain. I knew he didn't mean it, but it still hurt.

'That's not nice, Samuel. Don't call me that.'

'Weirdo. You can't make me sleep, weirdo.'

'Then you will need to sit on the bottom step until you are ready to sleep. Mia needs to go to bed.'

'I'm not going.'

'You are. Either you walk downstairs, or I carry you. What's it to be?'

'I'm not going.'

'I'll have to carry you, then.' I wrapped my arms around his waist as he punched and kicked me.

'Don't touch me, you weirdo. Get off.'

My heart was breaking for so many reasons. Firstly, because hearing those words was never easy. They made tears burn behind my eyes. But, also because I could see Samuel's mind screaming out to me. He was struggling. The words and actions could be translated into a child on the edge of not coping. Samuel's mind was battling against him, and he was reacting in the only way his brain would allow. This wasn't his choice.

I carried Samuel onto the step where he continued

to shout, scream and throw things for a long time. I don't know how long as I lost all concept of time whilst observing him from the next room. He had a bear for comfort which he hugged tightly, but he certainly didn't want comfort from me. If I spoke to him, or approached him, I was greeted with gritted teeth and a deep roar. So, I left him alone and took Mia to bed. I read her a story and hugged her tightly, needing that hug more than she could have realised. Amazingly, despite the noise, Mia was soon asleep.

Samuel stayed on the step for about an hour. When he quietened down, I asked him if he would like to go to bed. 'No.' He stayed there a little longer then walked up to his bedroom. He restarted his music, turned his sensory light back on and shut the door. All seemed quiet.

When I checked on Samuel a few minutes later he was fast asleep, his light balanced in both of his hands and he was lying in his toy basket. I lifted him onto his bed and left their bedroom, stopping by the wall on the landing to lean up against its cool surface. I sank down onto the floor, allowing the tears to flow freely down my cheeks. After some deep breaths, I went straight to bed, trying to process what had been a long day full of mixed emotions. I fell asleep feeling emotionally battered and very alone.

The secret life which we led was breaking me. Nobody knew how hard it was. Nobody asked how hard it was. I thought that maybe people suspected, but it was probably safer to pretend the secret life didn't exist. That way nobody else needed to get emotionally involved.

But we were there. Always there. Surviving.

Chapter 20

October 2014

After months and months of waiting, the day of Samuel's CAMHS appointment finally arrived. I had high hopes. This could be it. It could be the day I got some answers and support, which Samuel so desperately needed, and would hopefully help me to feel just a little less isolated.

Samuel seemed excited as we drove there, although it could have been nerves, and he didn't stop asking questions.

'What is this place called? I keep forgetting,' he asked.

'CAMHS.'

'Is it at the doctors?'

'No, but it isn't far away.'

'Who will I see?'

'A special nurse who specialises in helping children who struggle a bit at school.'

'What will they do to me?'

'She won't do anything. She'll just ask questions.'

'What will she ask me?'

'I don't know. I suppose she'll ask about school. And what you find difficult.'

'Will I have to do anything?'

'I don't think so. I don't know.'

My brain felt frazzled. I didn't really know how to answer any of these questions and felt like a failure as I couldn't mentally prepare him properly.

We arrived and walked into the reception area with ten minutes to spare.

'Hi. My son has an appointment at ten o'clock.'

She looked down at Samuel then back at me. 'Sorry, love, we don't treat children here. Who's your appointment with?'

A slight feeling of panic set in. 'CAMHS.'

'CAMHS moved a while ago. It's not too far from here, though. I'll write the address down for you.'

How could I have possibly made such a stupid mistake? The online address was wrong, and only then did I notice that it didn't match the address on the letter. Grabbing Samuel's hand, I hurriedly thanked the receptionist and made a hasty exit.

I reset the sat. nav. and we were off again, feeling less relaxed than I had been before. Thankfully, it wasn't too far away. We were getting near. I could see it. Just over that fence. But, how could we get in? I could see a car park, but there was a dirty great fence in the way.

Pulling my car over to the side of the road, I scanned the area. There was a small opening in the fence which we could walk through. Should I admit defeat and abandon the car? I quickly decided that, in that moment, the fine for parking in a permit-zone was irrelevant and a risk I was willing to take. We were both stressed, running late and neither of us were in the right frame of mind anymore for a long assessment.

The building was not like a doctor's surgery and didn't feel very welcoming from the outside. A blacked out and reinforced door with an intercom greeted us. I found this a little intimidating and really hoped that Samuel didn't sense my unease. He didn't. He was smiling and appeared to be excited: he thought he was on an adventure. When we were let in through the foreboding door, I informed the kind looking receptionist who we were. Her reassuring smile and calm voice enabled my stress levels to drop a little.

We were called in to see the nurse almost straight away. Samuel suddenly became nervous and went very quiet. *Don't be quiet, now, Samuel. Not now. Now is the time to be as hyperactive as you like,* I thought. The nurse said that he could either sit down, stand or play with the toys in the corner, whichever he felt comfortable with. He sat quietly in the chair. He would never usually choose that option, so why now? *Please, sweetie, show the mental-health nurse how you can't sit still or stop talking? No? Great.*

However, of course I didn't need to worry. Within just a few minutes Samuel was answering questions whilst fiercely swinging his legs back and forth in his chair. This was followed by bouncing and then sliding so far down in the chair that his head was on the seat and he was looking up at the ceiling. The whole time he had his rhino soft toy held against his face as he moved the fidgety beans in its legs between his fingers.

'Let's go right back to when Samuel was a baby. How was your pregnancy? Were there any problems?'

'No. No problems.'

'And was he full term?'

'Yes, forty-one weeks.'

'Any problems with the birth?'

'No, none at all.'

'Was he healthy? Did he need to go into special-care?'

'He was fine. We went home shortly after the birth.'

'Has he had any serious illnesses?'

'No, just recurring tonsillitis. He had them removed earlier this year.'

'How would you describe him as a baby? Did he appear to need more attention than other babies?'

'Err…'

What was he like? Why couldn't I remember? Samuel's first year had gone by in a blur of multi-tasking and child juggling. Losing Ben had been so hard, and yet I had still needed to be Mum. Having twins, I was constantly drowning in the combined needs of them both and the details were lost in a haze of nappies, breast-feeding, puréed vegetables and tears.

'I didn't really notice anything at the time, but I had twins. Everything was a bit manic.'

She scribbled some notes down, and I wondered if she had read between the lines and identified how I had struggled to cope during those early days.

'OK. Let's look at any family illnesses, now. Any history of mental illness?'

I hesitated. I knew that I had been depressed after I had given birth to the twins, but I had never seen a doctor. I pretended that I was coping, feeling ashamed to admit that I was drowning in a pit of treacle.

'No,' I said, still unable to admit to periods of depression.

The constant torrent of questions left my mind exhausted and drained, as if it was undergoing a spin-cycle in a washing machine, but it wasn't as stressful as I expected it to be. The fear, which coursed through my veins, was that my parenting would be dissected and judged, blaming me for Samuel's behaviours, but it wasn't like that. I had started the assessment feeling defensive and believing that I would be told that I had done something wrong in bringing him up. I always tried to bring the children up with love, care, respect and discipline when needed, but what if I had got it wrong? What if this expert saw that the problems originated from something I had done? Was it possible that I had really messed up this parenting thing? Nobody ever told me the right way to bring up a child, so it could be possible that I had got it completely wrong. These were very real fears of mine and, all of a sudden, I felt extremely vulnerable.

My parenting was never questioned. The conversation diverted towards talking about more recent events. I described his meltdowns in detail, and exactly what had triggered them. This was hard to talk about. I found the meltdowns the trickiest thing to deal with, physically and emotionally, and they had such a huge impact on the whole family.

After discussing various situations which had been difficult for Samuel, we started talking about which coping strategies I had put in place. I described the bedtime routine in lots of detail, and the sensory aids which helped him to sleep and calm down.

Hours had passed. If it was possible for a brain to hurt then mine was pounding. All of the behaviours were just part of our daily life but listing them all and discussing everything in quick succession settled heavily in my heart. My poor Samuel. Life was so hard for him. As we reached a natural end to the questioning, the nurse started summarising what her opinion was.

'OK, that was really thorough, thank you,' she said. She read back through some of her notes and the room fell silent for the first time. Samuel lay under my chair, rolling from side to side. I wanted to lift him up and squeeze him tightly. What would the nurse say?

'Most of Samuel's problems appear to be of a sensory nature. I think that this is a little more complex than simply pursuing a diagnosis for ADHD. His behaviour does indicate a difficulty in concentrating, and he can be hyperactive, but I would like the sensory issues dealt with before we tackle anything else. We may find that once Samuel isn't reacting to sensory stimulation in the classroom, he may be able to concentrate better.'

There it was. A sinking feeling immediately appeared inside me. Samuel probably had ADHD. My baby boy. The confirmation of this was surprisingly upsetting.

'So, what happens now?' I asked.

'I recommend seeing an occupational therapist. They can work with Samuel to develop a sensory diet to address his needs. Once the sensory processing is under control, we'll have a better idea of just how much the ADHD alone is affecting him.'

Relief flooded through me. I exhaled slowly, taking in what she had just said. There would be no ADHD diagnosis yet. Maybe it wouldn't even be necessary. The controversial label, which so many people would judge him – and me – for, could wait. And, just as importantly, I didn't need to engage with thoughts of medication. Not yet.

The nurse turned her attention back to Samuel, and she asked him questions whilst observing him playing. I sat quietly and watched him. Suddenly, I became fascinated by his actions with my new knowledge from the mental-health nurse. He balanced on the side of chairs, spun around, leant on walls and felt every toy in the room. He answered questions whilst lying on the floor, or twirling around, or playing with toys. Always on the move, but it was more than that. He wasn't simply hyperactive, dashing about the room, but there was always another element too. He was searching for sensory input. I felt like I was suddenly watching him with a new found understanding.

*

During the journey back to school, the realisation hit me that we still didn't have any diagnosis. I had previously felt relieved, being fearful of ADHD, but a diagnosis of any type could have opened doors to support. A diagnosis would have led to better understanding for me and school, and possibly funding for extra help in the classroom. We were almost no better off, regarding a need for support at school, than we were the day before. The practical advice and coping strategies, which I was desperately hoping for from CAMHS, never really materialised.

But we were one step closer.

Chapter 21

December 2014

Finishing work for the day, I did the usual dash across the car park ready to battle through rush-hour traffic. After-school club closed in fifteen minutes, and I was in a race against the clock to collect the children in time.

I always felt guilty arriving at the after-school club and realising that my children were the last to be collected again. As the weeks went by, the guilt seemed to be growing in intensity, especially as Samuel struggled to settle in the unstructured environment. I loved my job, and felt proud that I was demonstrating a hard work attitude for the children, but something had changed in my head and priorities were evolving.

Samuel seemed to be struggling more and more as each day passed. And, as he struggled, so did I. Neither of us were coping. I had made the difficult decision to see the GP again and had asked to be referred back to CAMHS. We needed help.

Some days I felt like I was drowning. Loving my job wasn't enough. The balance of work and home life was drastically tipped in favour of work, and I was struggling to stay afloat.

Some days my phone would ring as I worked. I wanted to ignore the quiet, but insistent, buzzing in my bag, but I knew that it could be school. One of the children was sick. One of them had had a fall. One of them was asleep on the classroom floor with a raging temperature. One of them had run into a door handle and split their head open. One of them had something in their eye and couldn't see. One of them had a sensory meltdown and had thrashed out and hit a member of staff. The temptation was to not answer the phone. *Please, let me do my job. Don't ask me to walk out again. Please.* However, I always answered. Then I had the dilemma of either being a responsible mum or being responsible for my students.

Evenings were a tricky balance. Once I had the realisation that I had started to consider my children as being time-consuming, I realised that I had a real problem. It sickened me to think that I hurried their time to make time for my work. They didn't care if I had a list of work to complete, and they shouldn't have had to care. They deserved my complete time and attention. On the nights when Samuel chose not to sleep, I didn't do any work in the evening. The work didn't disappear when it was ignored, but it started growing and growing until it was suffocating.

Was this really the way I wanted to live? In a never-ending spin-cycle? Dragging my children with me whether they wanted to be there or not?

Something had to give.

Could I really give it all up? No. I loved my job and needed the money. I couldn't imagine myself doing any other work. But maybe I could significantly reduce my hours. Step down from Head of Department and just concentrate on teaching. Financially, it would be difficult but not impossible. When I had first started my job, I would never have imagined me making this decision. However, maybe it was something that I should have considered in the first place when I started work. Making time for me and my children could be the best decision I had ever made.

I would be able to attend meetings at Samuel's school to discuss how he was progressing and coping. I could sit with my children and help with homework in a less rushed way. They would no longer be dragged to meetings with me and be expected to wait outside the room for me to finish. Instead, we could go to the park and play.

My main job would be Mum. The single most important job I could ever dream of having the privilege to do. It was possible that without Samuel's complex needs influencing my day-to-day life, I may not have even considered that as an option. I would have carried on trying to juggle all the components of my life. Both children would benefit, though, if I could just stop and breathe.

Chapter 22

December 2014

Robin had continued to be a massive part of my life despite the fact that we rarely saw each other. The stolen moments when we managed to lie in each other's arms made everything worth it. He had become my world. Alongside my children, he was my reason to breathe in and out. He was my future, and I longed for the day when his work would ease for long enough for us to become one. I knew it would happen. I just had to be patient.

Every evening, for three years, I had sat with him whilst he worked, albeit on Skype, and I imagined what it would be like to actually sit next to him instead. To be close enough to hear his breathing and catch his scent in the air. I longed for it every day, but our evenings online together were a close second. The chaos of the day gently drifted away behind a protective bubble which swelled around us as we became lost in our own little world. It meant everything to me.

When he was able to visit, he slotted so naturally into my family that it was like he had always been there. The children adored him, and my life felt complete. A magnetised pull drew me towards him, and I felt something I didn't often experience: pure euphoria. Every day with him felt like a holiday and mundane tasks became exciting, because he was there.

Then, when he went home, a part of me broke every time and left with him. It never got easier. As he said goodbye, to return to his other life, I would hold him: breathing in the scent of his neck, merging my body with his in our last embrace, savouring every sensation and storing them in my memory to be drawn on later when I would be alone again. Every time, I fell apart a little, knowing it would be months before I saw him again. But, I accepted it, because it was either that or lose him. And I couldn't lose him. So, I picked myself up and waited for the next phone call. The next email. The next Skype call.

Robin had always emailed many times a day. *How are you? How did you sleep? How are the children? Have I told you today that I love you?* Every time I heard the joyous ping coming from my phone my heart raced, and I rushed to read it feeling as excited as I had three years before. However, one evening the email was very different. I wasn't ready.

Sweetie, I don't think I can do this anymore...

And that was it. My heart shattered irreparably within a second of reading those words. A tight squeezing around my chest. A blade, slicing down my throat. A burning in my eyes. And my world came crashing down around me.

You're finishing with me? Over email? Seriously?

Denial. He wouldn't do that to me. He loved me.

I'm sorry. I'll call in a bit.

I fell on to my bed and cried; silently sobbing as my heart and soul dissolved around me, leaving nothing but pain. It was over.

I couldn't do any of it without him. Our little bubble, which offered me more protection from the world's forces than he would ever understand, had gone forever. Nothing would ever be the same again.

Chapter 23

February 2015

The difficult decision had been made to apply for an Education and Health Care Plan for Samuel. The EHCP would provide advice for the school to follow to assist his education and necessary funding to pay for his 1:1 help in class. I had a meeting scheduled with Mr Hart, the school SENCO, and I had arrived at the school feeling prepared to discuss all of Samuel's difficulties and challenges at school.

Mr Hart was waiting in the reception for me.

'Hi, Amelia. You OK?'

'Yeah, I'm good, thanks.'

I signed the visitors' book and took a badge. Mr Hart led the way to an office where the computer was already loaded up with Samuel's forms.

'Right, I've completed the first page, with personal details, already. I'll ask you what you want to put into each section, and I'll type. We can add in bits from old referral forms as we go through it.' He scrolled to the next page of the form.

'OK. First question. What are Samuel's positives?'

Mr Hart was poised ready at the keyboard. I stared at him and froze. His positives? We had had a particularly exhausting week, and I had attended the meeting armed with lists of relevant challenges that Samuel faces every day. But positives? Why would nothing come to me?

Instantly appalled with myself, I struggled to come up with any positive information that would help his assessment. In a panic, I tried to dismiss all the difficult areas that I had been so ready to discuss and to think of something positive. Anything.

The first words that came out of my mouth filled me with shame. However, in that moment of sleep deprivation and feeling mentally drained, I could think of nothing.

'Can we come back to it? I can't think of anything.'

It made me cringe. It made me hate myself. It made my heart feel like a lead weight in my chest. It made me want to scream at myself in anger for being such a negative mother in that moment.

Mr Hart smiled. 'Of course. If you like, I can send you the form and you can fill that part in later when you've had time to think.'

I thanked him weakly, disgusted that I had fallen at the first hurdle, and we moved on to the next section of the form.

As soon as I was home, with the children in bed, I loaded up the form on my laptop and started to answer the question in peace. Of course, I knew exactly how to answer it. It was so obvious. So easy.

So, why couldn't I think of those wonderful, inspirational and beautiful positives when asked to?

It made me re-evaluate how I approached each day. What a shock to realise that I was so in tune with supporting his everyday challenges, and so consumed by the daily meltdowns and shutdowns, that I had subconsciously assumed that my capacity for supporting him was limited to making the difficult parts better.

I felt disgusted and struggled to understand how I had allowed myself to fail him on this point. I never thought of myself as failing him, but, in a way, that's exactly what I was doing in some instances. Nobody could have fought more for support. Nobody could have defiantly justified his actions more. Nobody could have researched his challenges more to try to understand them better. In those areas, I was winning. So much so that there was nothing left to notice the sparkling, colourful, fantastically wonderful positives that were peeping out at me just below the surface.

I started to type as my mind cleared, and Samuel's character burst into technicolour, clear for me to see. He was kind. So kind. He looked after his soft toys as if they were alive. There was so much love towards them, and he handled them with care in a nurturing way. He was affectionate and showed me so much love it made my heart melt every day.

His memory astounded me. He could recall things from almost any point in his life with alarming detail: remembering clothes we all wore, what was eaten and what was said. Random facts seemed to imprint into his memory.

Attention to detail was always observed. *Where's*

Wally books became a competitive game as I tried to beat him to find the hidden characters. He usually won.

He often developed a type of hyper-focus when engaging in computer-based activities or constructing something out of Lego. He admitted that he wasn't aware of anyone, or anything, around him in those moments and could concentrate for hours. I pondered for a moment about whether there could be a way to hone this skill better as he got older.

In his calmer moments, he would ask me if I needed help. If I was cooking, or gardening, he would be there. If I was carrying heavy bags, he would try to take one from me.

I started to type and found that I couldn't stop. These were the points that should always stand out the most, and I knew that I needed to make a conscious effort to see these positives before his challenges. He was so much more than the little tornado that I too often saw him for.

Chapter 24

March 2015

I woke up to the sound of shrieking at six o'clock in the morning. Out of habit, I checked my phone expecting an email from Robin. It wasn't there, and I remembered, with renewed despair, that he didn't send me morning emails anymore. Those days had gone.

With a painful sigh, I got out of bed to investigate the noise. Samuel was in his bedroom, clothes pulled out of his drawers and scattered everywhere, and he was standing on his bed completely naked except for a large grin.

'What's going on, Samuel?'

'I'm deciding what to wear.'

It took a few seconds for the sleepy fog to clear in my head, and then I realised. My heart sank. It was Comic Relief Day at school.

Comic Relief was exciting for most children, but for a child who couldn't regulate his emotions it was like waking up on Christmas Day. The prospect of mufti day, cake sales and whatever other amusing activities the school had in store was too much for Samuel. He was very excited and very hyper.

Samuel entered the school wearing his red clothes and red nose, looking like all the other children to anybody who couldn't read the signs. But I'd noticed them. His lack of communication. His eyes, which darted around, immediately took in everything as he drank in the other children's colourful outfits and red noses. The way he clutched his rhino against his cheek, craving the soft material against his skin.

I stopped and stared at him. Should I leave him here to a potentially impossible day? Was that fair? Or, should I phone in sick and take him home? No. Samuel had been looking forward to it. It wasn't fair to restrict his fun.

The day dragged. I kept looking at my phone, expecting a call from school, but there was nothing. At three o'clock, I drove to school wondering if we had maybe got away with it this time. Maybe Samuel had coped with the bright colours and silly activities that had been planned. Maybe it was all OK.

It wasn't. As I approached the school door, I could see Samuel with his face pushed against the glass, waiting for me. As soon as he saw me approaching, he jumped up to reach the door release button and ran out of the school building, straight past me and towards the road.

I ran after him with panic surging within. The road was busy. Parents were arriving to collect their children, and I could see that Samuel wasn't capable, in that moment, of understanding that. He would run straight into the road, oblivious of the cars approaching from both directions. My blood ran cold.

Just as Samuel reached the edge of the road, I caught him. I knew not to talk. He needed all sensory stimulation to cease, including my voice. Instead, I wrapped my arms around Samuel and held him tightly against my body. He fought against me, grunting, kicking and punching, but I held tight We'd been there before, many times, and I knew that the only thing I could do was to keep him safe. He would eventually calm down; we were in it for the long haul.

Meltdowns like that had started to happen more frequently, and I'd been in that position, on the edge of a road, too many times. Being drawn into these meltdowns was scary and traumatic, seeing my child lose all sense of self-control like that. They were also dangerous. All I could do was ride it out, suppressing the panic inside me.

I tried not to look at anyone passing by. I had caught the eye-rolling and staring before, but these situations were so consuming that I couldn't dwell on what others were thinking. Did they think he just needed a good talking to? A smack? I didn't care what they thought. My survival instincts took over and I concentrated on just keeping Samuel safe until the moment passed. This wasn't a child feeling cross and wanting his own way; there was a small child with no regard for his own safety and just needed to run.

Generally, meltdowns felt very isolating. Who wanted to get involved with somebody else's child who had lost control? Nobody would choose that. Nobody ever helped. However, I gradually became aware that something was different.

As I sat on the edge of the road, with my arms wrapped around Samuel's little body which was lashing out in distress, people positioned themselves around, so he couldn't get hurt by a passing car. People were ready to catch him if he escaped my arms. Somebody came up behind me and placed her hand on my shoulder.

'I've got your back. I'm here behind you,' she said.

A lump was forming in my throat. It was the first time anybody had ever done that in the street. It helped. Samuel still fought against me in a battle to break free and run off down the street, and I was still primarily the one trying to be in control of that, but I knew that I wasn't alone. What a difference that made.

It took about thirty minutes for Samuel to calm down. If the people supporting me got bored in that time, they didn't show it. They stood firm: my silent guard. As Samuel started to calm down he pushed into my embrace, and I supported his weight. He was emotionally and physically drained. I knew it wouldn't be long.

Samuel's TA Mrs Peters was standing nearby. 'Where's Mia?' I asked, feeling like a crap parent. How had I not asked that question before? Mia could have been anywhere.

'She's in school. I'll get her.'

'Thank you,' I said, weakly. Also exhausted, I wrapped my arms around Samuel and guided him further away from the road and sat down, resting my head on his. The smell of his hair was calming.

'Are you ready to go home?' I asked him. Samuel silently shook his head.

'OK. That's OK, sweetie. We can stay here for a bit.'

Mia nervously approached from behind. I smiled encouragingly at her. She hated seeing Samuel like this.

'Hey, Mia. Are you alright?'

'Yes. Is Samuel OK?' she asked, quietly.

'Yes, he's fine, now. Could you do me a favour, please?' I shifted my weight, unwrapped an arm from Samuel's shoulder and managed to free my keys from my pocket. 'Can you get Samuel's blanket from the car, please?'

Mia ran off to the car, desperate to help. My heart melted. It wasn't fair that she had to experience this, too. She came back with Samuel's blanket, and I wrapped it tightly around him. I turned to the people in the road behind me and smiled gratefully.

'Thank you so much. We're OK now.'

'You sure?' a voice from behind me asked.

'Yes. He's alright.'

And they dispersed in all directions without a word. A reassuring hand squeezed my shoulder. I don't know who it was.

The blanket helped. Five minutes passed, and I could feel that Samuel had completely surrendered. His little body hung limply in my arms. Without a word, I stood up, lifted him into my arms and began the struggle to walk the short distance to my car.

Driving home, I allowed tears to fall freely. *Thank you*, I thought, over and over again. *Thank you.*

*

I felt drained when I got home. Something needed to change. I had been waiting for three months to hear from CAMHS following another referral from my

GP. Why hadn't they got in touch?

I called the GP surgery.

'I was told in December that my son was being referred to CAMHS, but I haven't heard anything. Can I just check that the referral went off OK, please?'

'Let me put you through to the lady who deals with referrals,' the receptionist said, and I waited.

'Good morning. How can I help you?'

'Hi. I just want to check that my son's referral to CAMHS went off. I haven't heard anything from them, and it's been a few months now.'

'Can I have your son's name and date of birth, please?'

I gave her the details and waited.

'A referral was sent to CAMHS in December. I think it's a good idea if I resend it off to them today.'

'Resend it?' I was confused. If the referral had been sent, why would they resend it?

'But, if they already have the referral, and it's waiting to be processed, could we be risking Samuel being bumped to the bottom of the queue again by resending it? Especially if the new referral has today's date on it? Maybe I should just check with CAMHS what's going on, first.'

'No, I think it's sensible to resend the referral if you haven't heard anything yet.'

Doubt crept into my mind. 'Was the original referral definitely sent?'

'Yes. It won't hurt to resend it, though.'

I thanked her, said goodbye and immediately called CAMHS, explaining the situation to the lady on the phone.

'I've checked through all of the referrals which have been processed, and the list which are waiting for appointments still, and we haven't received one for your son.'

'It was sent in December. Are you sure?' Anger and frustration burned like a fire inside my stomach.

'I've looked twice. We definitely haven't received anything from your GP.'

How could the referrals lady at the surgery forget something as important as this? My son's mental health desperately needed treating, and she forgot? She had one job. Just one. When referrals came from the GP, her job was to complete them and send them off to the relevant health team. Easy, right?

Any last shred of hope I may have been clinging onto over the whole system had simply melted away.

Chapter 25

April 2015

Walking out of work, I checked my phone. *Damn.* There was a voicemail from school waiting for me. Reluctantly, I listened.

'Hello, Amelia. I've been asked to give you a call before you arrive to collect the children. Samuel has had a difficult day. He's refusing to stay in the classroom and is kicking a ball around the hall. We just wanted to warn you, in case he tries to run again when you get here. It might be best if you come to the main entrance as we can keep the door locked until you're ready to leave.'

I groaned and felt my heartbeat quicken. I was tired and didn't feel ready for a battle, but I started to hurry. There was no point delaying the inevitable.

At school, I went to the main entrance, amidst a cloud of dread, wondering if Samuel had managed to calm down. The receptionist smiled apologetically at me.

'Hi, Amelia. I'll just go and let them know you're here. Mia's waiting for you, too.'

'Thanks. Has there been any change? What's Samuel doing?'

'I'm sorry, I'm not sure. Hang on a minute and I'll find out what the situation is.'

She disappeared through the office and into the school. Nervously, I waited, unsure what I was about to face. Would Samuel refuse to leave? Would I be carrying him out of the building? Or, would he make a run for it? The main door was locked, so I should be able to control the situation. Possibly. In reality, I never felt like I was controlling the situation. I just rode each wave, desperately clinging on by my fingernails, and hoping I wouldn't get sucked under the current.

I heard him before I saw him. An ear-piercing scream which cut through me and made my heart pound. *Here we go...*

His face appeared at the locked door which separated the reception area from the main school. There was a wildness to his eyes as if the real Samuel wasn't there anymore. I was looking the disorder straight in the eye, seeing its raw, painful depths. It had consumed Samuel, and he was fighting, but its pull was too strong.

He jumped up to reach the door release button, and I braced myself for impact, positioning myself in front of the door. He ran, straight towards the button to open the main door, but the receptionist had remembered to override it before she left. Samuel repeatedly hit the button, ignoring me, and getting more worked up with every failed attempt. I reached towards him, trying to guide him away from the door, but he roughly pushed me away and a primal scream erupted from him. I felt helpless. The receptionist hurriedly returned.

'I've locked both doors, Amelia,' she said in a low voice. 'We'll direct everyone else away from the main entrance. He's safe here until he calms down.'

I thanked her, but my attention was quickly drawn back to Samuel. He had heard everything and was hitting the door release button hard, trying to force it open. Each failed attempt got him more distressed. He then turned to the door which would take him back into the school. He threw himself against the door again and again; a deep scream accompanying every failed attempt to escape the confinements of the reception area. He felt trapped. He *was* trapped. And he was getting increasingly more distressed with every second that passed.

Oh God, maybe containing him in this small area is a really bad idea, I thought, as Samuel threw himself from one door to the next. But what was the alternative? Open the door to the school and allow him to run through and get out another door? He would almost certainly run into the street outside, or just keep running further and further away. And what if I caught him? What would I do? Restrain him for an hour until he calmed down with him hitting, kicking and biting both of us the whole time? No. We were safer where we were, even if his temporary imprisonment was distressing him more.

Samuel moved away from the door, and his eyes darted around the reception area. *What are you thinking?* I didn't have to wonder for long, as he pushed past me and picked up a small rubbish bin. Before I could stop him, he had hurled it against the glass door. With a clatter it fell to the floor with no damage. Samuel went to retrieve it.

'No, Samuel,' I pleaded, and I wrapped my arms around him tightly. He pulled hard against my arms and then leant forward to bite me. I kept my arms there, breathing through the pain.

The headteacher, Mrs Allan, let herself through the door and relocked it, speaking to me in a whisper.

'Where's your car?'

'In the staff car park,' I answered.

'If I help you move him, we could safely get him through the school and to your car.'

What? How on earth would that help?

'What do we do when we get to my car, though?'

'Moving him away from here may be enough to calm him down. I can help you carry him into your car. He'll be safer there.'

My head was spinning. Samuel was in full meltdown, and she was suggesting getting him out of the school building and into my car? What then? I would drive off with Samuel still throwing, kicking and trying to escape the car? Why was she suggesting that?

'I can't drive with him like this. It's too dangerous.'

'But he may calm down when we move him away from here.'

'And he may not,' I snapped. I wasn't willing to risk it.

'OK. Do you want me to stay with you?'

'Thanks, but no. I think it's better if it's just me. I don't want to overwhelm him any more.'

'Of course. I'll be the other side of the door, though. Shout if you need me.'

'Thank you.' I hoped she realised how grateful I was.

She retreated through the door. Samuel's attack against me was getting stronger, and I could see faint ribbons of blood on my arms where he had scratched me.

'Get off me, you weirdo.' They were the first words he had spoken. The words seemed to come from deep inside, throaty and gritty.

'But you were throwing things.'

'I won't.'

My arms and shins were hurting. 'OK. But if you throw anything, I will hold you again.'

As I released him he made a run for the door and threw his whole body-weight against it. The door didn't move, and Samuel screamed so loudly my blood ran cold. I watched him, unsure what my next move would be. Would he calm down more quickly if I left him to burn out? Or did I need to intervene again? I had no idea what to do for the best.

And then, as if in answer to my inner turmoil, he stood facing the door into the school and thrust his head into the glass with a sickening thud. I watched in horror as he smashed his head into the door again and again in quick succession.

'No, Samuel,' I pleaded, and ran across the room towards him, wrapping my arms around him again, and pulling him towards the ground.

'You weirdo. Get off me.'

I didn't, knowing that he would fight against me but didn't have the strength to escape. I could hold him safely. Tears started to burn in my eyes.

I held him like that for a long time. Eventually the fighting eased until he lay exhausted in my arms. I relaxed my grip and started to stroke his hair. It was nearly over. Mrs Allan released the door lock and quietly entered.

'You OK?'

I nodded. 'Would it be possible to get a water for Samuel, please? We're nearly ready to leave.'

She smiled and walked away, returning a few minutes later with a tall glass of water. Samuel finished it in one go.

'Mia's by the back door, near your car. Do you want to try and move, now?'

I stood up. Samuel didn't move. 'Do you want me to carry you?'

Samuel nodded, and I lifted him onto my hip, struggling against his weight. He nestled his head into my neck and closed his eyes. Once in the car, he pulled his blanket over his face and immediately slept.

Something had to change. There was no way we could carry on like that. It was time to call CAMHS. When I returned home, I called CAMHS immediately. After explaining how Samuel was hurting himself, they decided that he had successfully qualified for an urgent appointment. The words sank inside me, churning my stomach and leaving me with a queasy sadness. When I planned my little family I never imagined I would be in a position where I would be asking for urgent CAMHS appointments.

However, we were one step nearer to getting the help we so desperately needed.

Chapter 26

May 2015

Mia seemed unusually quiet as we left school. Something was bothering her.

'You OK, sweetie?' I asked.

'Yes.'

'You're very quiet.'

Mia took my hand and squeezed it. 'I don't want to say anything here. Can I tell you later?'

'Of course.' Mia sometimes reacted like this when she had argued with a friend. I assumed that she'd had a bad day, we'd chat later and it would all blow over the next day. It always did. I bent down and kissed the top of Mia's head.

'Talk whenever you're ready to,' I said.

Later, when Samuel was glued to the television screen, completely lost in his Minecraft world, I went and sat next to Mia on her bed and wrapped her up in my arms.

'What's up, beautiful?' I asked.

She hesitated, looked me in the eye then looked away.

'It's OK, Mia. Whatever it is, you can talk to me about it.'

'Thomas said something to me this morning.'

'OK. What did he say?'

'It wasn't very nice.'

She snuggled into my side, resting her head on me, and I played with her hair, waiting for her to be ready to confide in me. It only took a few seconds.

'Samuel was under my desk. Thomas said that he was weird and annoying. He called him an idiot.' Her voice shook.

'Oh, sweetie, that must have been horrible to hear.'

'It was.' I could hear that she was crying, and my heart broke. I held her whilst she wept.

'Do you know why he said those things about Samuel?' I asked.

'Because he's horrible. He always says horrid things about him.'

'No, sweetie. He isn't horrible. It's just that he doesn't understand. I imagine that nobody has ever explained why Samuel behaves differently sometimes. What did you say to Thomas when he said those things?'

'I said that Samuel isn't weird.'

'Good. Because he isn't.' I held her tightly as her crying started to ease and then spoke gently. 'Samuel is different. We're all different. We all have different ways we behave. Do you understand why Samuel sometimes hides under the table or runs around the school noisily?'

'He finds school difficult.'

'Yes, he does. Thomas is able to ignore the noises in the classroom, and the wind outside the window, and birds singing in the trees, and the people moving around the classroom, and the smell of the teacher's perfume. Samuel can't. He notices everything. And it all gets too much, and he gets hyper. Or, sometimes he hides to make everything go away. That doesn't make him weird. Different, yes. But not weird.'

'Thomas won't listen if I tell him that, though.'

'No.' I sighed. 'It's hard for him to understand when he doesn't feel like that himself. He's probably never met anyone like Samuel before. You need to try to not get upset by it, though.'

Mia hugged me tightly. 'OK, Mummy.'

Becoming aware of the time, I kissed the top of her head and left the room. A friend from work, Sophie, was taking me out later in an attempt to cheer me up. Since Robin had finished with me, I had become withdrawn, isolating myself from the pain in the world. Sophie correctly interpreted my lack of contact, realising that I was in a bad place, and she insisted that we should go out.

Going out always filled with the same creeping dread. Would I actually manage to successfully get the children sorted before it was time to leave the house? It felt like an impossible challenge every time.

Things were going to plan. Dinner was eaten on time and the children were calm and sprawled in front of the TV. I tentatively crept towards Samuel, a little afraid to mention the dreaded 'bedtime' word in case it provoked the kind of crazy reaction that I really didn't have time for.

'Bedtime, both of you,' I said.

Mia got up to go upstairs, but Samuel dived under a blanket and sat very, very still.

'No, come on. It's bedtime.'

Nothing. No movement at all. *Now you choose to practise the skill of sitting still? No, no, no… not tonight…*

Then, suddenly, he stood up and silently walked towards the stairs. I'd done it! I had control and the voice of authority. Hurrah for my parenting skills!

'I'm only going to go to sleep if you make me a den to sleep in.'

Damn.

'We're not doing dens tonight, sweetie. It's just sleep time, now.'

'But I can't go to sleep tonight without a den. I'll be scared. I'll be safer in a den.'

'Oh, I want a den, too,' said Mia.

'Mia! That's not helping,' I said, irritably.

'Well, why shouldn't I get a den, too? If Samuel gets one, then I want one.'

I opened my mouth to protest, then closed it again. *Pick your battles.* So, we took clothes pegs and found blankets, and we constructed something above both of their beds which didn't quite look like dens. Unsure whether they met the den standard of approval, I congratulated us heartily on our fantastic den building and hoped that I sounded convincing enough. It worked.

With a sigh of relief, they both fell asleep. It took me five minutes to get ready, and I remembered back to before I had children when I would spend all afternoon preparing for a night out.

The babysitter arrived. With a reluctant sigh, I left the house. If I was completely honest with myself, I didn't want to go out. I didn't want to cheer up.

I just wanted Robin.

Chapter 27

June 2015

It was Samuel's bedtime. I had sat next to him on the bed, ready to read him a story. Samuel was lying down and fidgeting a bit whilst trying to get comfortable. Suddenly, he sat upright and started shaking his head and grabbing at his ear with a look of horror on his face.

'Something went in my ear.'

'What? What went in your ear?'

'I don't know. I just felt it go in.'

'Are you sure? Can you still feel it?'

'Yes. It hurts.' He was still frantically shaking his head.

'Right. Stop shaking and come into the bathroom. I'll have a look.'

I wasn't overly concerned. Surely nothing could have fallen into his ear whilst he lay on the bed? Unless… I felt a cold shudder sweep over me. Could it have been a spider?

Samuel followed me into the bathroom, still shaking his head.

'I can feel it in there.'

I got my phone out of my pocket and turned its torch-light on.

'OK, you need to stand really still whilst I look.'

'Will it hurt?'

I could see his anxieties growing.

'No. I'm just looking.'

I shone the light into his ear but struggled to see down the bendy ear canal. Gently, I moved his head to a different position.

'Ow. It hurts,' he said.

'Sorry, Sammy. It may have just moved. Let me look again.'

And then I saw it. Deep inside his ear, a white dot sparkled in the light.

'Oh my god, you were right. There's something there.' Overwhelmingly relieved that it wasn't a spider, I adjusted the light and turned his head slightly, so I could get a better look.

'What is it?' Samuel asked.

'I don't know. It's white and shiny. Are you sure you didn't put anything in your ear?'

'I didn't do it!'

'OK.' Could I get it out? No, it was in far too deep. My mind raced, as I tried to figure out what on Earth I needed to do about it. *Can it wait until the morning? We can go to the doctors when they open*, I thought. Probably not. What if it was doing damage to the inside of his ear whilst moving about in there? No. It needed to be sorted immediately.

'We need to go and see a doctor to try and get it out,' I said.

'What, now?' His eyes became large and panic stricken.

'Yes. Go and get some socks on then come downstairs.'

I ran downstairs where Mia was watching TV and explained the situation, instructing her to get her shoes and coat on. Samuel had just arrived with his socks and dressing gown on. I went to tell him to change it for his coat but stopped myself. It wasn't important, and he probably felt comforted by his Gruffalo dressing gown. He needed all the comfort he could get.

Mia got her coat on excitedly. Bedtime had been abandoned in favour of an adventure. Samuel looked less enthusiastic. I gave him a hug.

'It's OK, don't worry. They'll be able to get it out easily.'

'How? What will they do?' he asked.

'I'm not sure, but they probably have something that will be able to grab it to pull it out.'

Silently, he rubbed Rhino's ear on his cheek: a sign that he was worried. *Please let this be straightforward*, I thought.

*

We arrived at the hospital and made our way to the minor injuries department with Samuel gripping my hand tightly. Amazingly, there was only one other patient before us in the waiting room. I registered Samuel at the reception desk, then we sat down to wait.

A door opened, and an elderly nurse with short, silvery hair came over to us, smiling.

'Samuel?' she said.

Samuel buried his face in my arm.

'Yes, this is Samuel. He's a bit nervous,' I said.

'Oh, we're not scary. The first thing I need to do is just talk to you and Mum. Is that OK?'

I stood up, gently pulled Samuel to his feet and followed the nurse into the triage room. I explained what had happened, and she looked inside Samuel's ear.

'I can see it. That shouldn't be a problem. I can get that out easily enough.'

Samuel whimpered and pulled away from the nurse.

'It's nothing to worry about, m'duck. I'll pop a special straw into your ear, and it will suck up whatever's in there. It won't hurt.'

Samuel didn't look convinced, and my panic started to grow. We were led through a different door and towards a bed where Samuel was asked to lie down. He lay with his ear completely covered by the pillow.

'That's not going to work, Sammy. You can't lie on that side. How will the nurse get the thing out your ear?' I said.

'Don't want her to.'

'I know, but she has to. It can't stay there.'

I gently turned him over, and his hand flew to his ear, covering it. This wasn't going to be easy.

The nurse came back, holding a threatening-looking instrument, explaining how it would remove the object from his ear. Samuel wasn't listening. He was staring at the suction device with a look of sheer panic on his face. My heart was pounding heavily against my chest as my fear also intensified.

'He has sensory processing difficulties, and he's very scared,' I said, breathlessly.

'It's OK. I'll go slowly.'

For any child, having a suction device inserted into the ear is a scary experience. For a child with heightened anxiety and an inability to process sensory stimulation in their environment, it is nothing short of traumatising. We were told that it would be a simple procedure and take just a few minutes. They weren't anticipating my little tornado, however.

As soon as the suction device was presented to him, he panicked. The closer it got to his ear, the more scared he became. The feeling of it entering his ear took him close to his limit of what he could cope with. Then it was turned on. The screams that ensued could be heard across the whole department. He had entered full meltdown.

As he screamed and fought against anybody that came near him it was obvious that they would be unsuccessful. The nursing staff persevered for a little longer, with back-up arriving to help try and hold him, but he became more and more distressed. Mia watched on, horrified, and broke down into sobs of despair as she watched her brother completely losing control.

To my relief, Mia was led away by a nurse. I tried to hold Samuel still, but he fought against me with all his strength. I longed for it to be over.

Finally, the nurse removed all the equipment from the bed-space and put a hand on Samuel's shoulder.

'It's OK, Samuel. I've stopped now.'

Relief consumed me – even if it was short lived. The unidentified, offending object still had to come out, but for now we could breathe. Tears burned my eyes as I tried to gain control of my emotions whilst comforting Samuel.

'What now?' I asked, terrified of the answer.

'It's up against his eardrum, so it's giving him a bit of pain which isn't helping his state of mind. I'm going to make an appointment with the ENT clinic here, tomorrow morning. Their doctors may have a few different tricks up their sleeves to get it out of his ear.'

OK. And breathe. That was it for the night. Thankfully, I pulled Samuel over the bed into my arms. At first, he resisted, but I coaxed him with promises that it was all over for the night. The nurse went off to phone through for an emergency appointment, and I held Samuel's exhausted body as his breathing gradually slowed down.

An appointment was made for the next morning, and we left the hospital with all of us feeling completely traumatised. Not for the first time, I wished I could call Robin. I needed his company and his understanding. I longed to hear his reassuring voice telling me how everything would be OK. The pain of those memories chipped yet another fragment of my fractured heart away, and I sank into the familiar pool of pain which so often engulfed me.

*

The following day, I took a very subdued Samuel into the ENT clinic. As we waited for over an hour in a very busy hospital, I could see his anxiety levels creeping up again. When we were finally called into the treatment room, his hands were shaking.

'Hello there, young man. What can I help you with today?' the doctor asked.

Samuel didn't speak.

'He has something in his ear. We're not sure what it is, or how it got there, but it's right up against his eardrum. We tried to get it removed at the minor injuries clinic, but Samuel has sensory processing difficulties and had a meltdown from the sound and feel of the suction equipment.'

'That sounds like a horrible experience for you, Samuel,' the doctor said. 'Shall we see if we can make it any better?'

Samuel sat on my lap with his hands over his ears, and his eyes firmly shut. I smiled weakly at the doctor.

'I don't know how successful this is going to be. He's so scared,' I said in a hushed voice.

The doctor gently laid a hand on Samuel's arm.

'Samuel? Can you move your hands away for a minute, please?' I just want to talk to you. Look. I haven't got anything in my hands.'

Samuel opened his eyes and looked at the doctor, distrusting and afraid. As the doctor slowly raised his hands to reveal how empty they were, Samuel let his hands slip down his face and away from his ears.

'I'm not going to do anything until you say I can. OK? You have the control today. Do you want to have a go with my clever toy? It's used to get things out of ears. You can have a go with it first if you want to?'

Samuel was interested. He leant forward a little to get a better look and then nodded.

'Good boy. Now, look what this can do. I'm going

to do it on my hand. Then you can do it on my hand. It makes a bit of noise, but you can turn it on if you want to?'

The doctor pointed to a button, and Samuel pressed it. A whirring motor sound started up.

'Oh, it's quieter than the one last night,' I said.

'Of course. I have all the best equipment. Is the noise OK?' he asked Samuel. Samuel didn't answer but also didn't withdraw.

'This little tube goes into your ear – it doesn't hurt – then it gently sucks the thing in your ear, so I can quickly get it out. It will only take a few seconds. Here, try it on my hand.'

Samuel took it from the doctor and sucked the skin on his hand. The doctor laughed.

'It tickles. Try it on your hand. It feels funny,' the doctor said.

Samuel experimented with the devise: gently brushing it over his hand and then pushing it a bit harder.

'Shall we have a listen to what it sounds like next to your ear? I won't put it in, yet.'

Samuel fiercely shook his head. My hopes sank desperately.

'You tell me when to stop. I'm going to turn it on, all the way over here, and then slowly move towards you. Tell me if you need me to stop moving, and I will freeze until you say I can move a bit closer. Does that sound OK?'

No answer. I turned Samuel to face me.

'Sammy, it has to come out. It can't stay in there. The nice doctor is being very lovely and isn't going to scare you. OK?' I said. Samuel looked terrified. My heart ached. 'Please, sweetie. Let's just try.'

Very slowly, Samuel nodded again.

'That's it. You're such a brave boy,' I said, holding him close to me.

The doctor moved a few centimetres closer.

'Stop!' Samuel shouted.

Good as his word, he stopped and waited. After about ten seconds, he said, 'Shall we go a little further? Tell me when to stop again.'

Samuel didn't answer, but again he didn't pull away. The doctor moved a little closer.

'Stop!'

Without a word, the doctor stopped, waited a few seconds and then carried on. He stopped a few more times before speaking to Samuel. 'I'm close to your ear, now. I'm going to just let it gently touch the outside of your ear.'

'No, I'm scared.'

'I know you are, but I'm not going to put it in your ear, OK? Just the outside, and only for a second.'

Samuel was quietly sobbing by this point but didn't say anything. The doctor took this as a green light and allowed the side of the tube to gently touch his ear.

And that's when the screaming started. Regardless of how sensitive the doctor was to Samuel's needs, it was all still too much for him, and Samuel started rocking back and forth in the chair with his hands over his ears and big eyes staring straight ahead.

'I'm scared, I'm scared, I'm scared…' he repeated, over and over again. And I was crying, too; our hot tears combined as they soaked through to our clothes, and I held him so tightly my arms ached.

The poor doctor placed the equipment down and surveyed the scene.

'I can't carry on. I'm sorry. I don't want to be the person who traumatises him. I can't do that to Samuel.'

I nodded slowly, not daring to ask what this meant. He answered my unspoken question.

'I'm going to book Samuel in tomorrow morning, for it to be removed under general anaesthetic.'

I buried my face in Samuel's hair. *No.*

'It's the only way I can get it out, and I can't leave it in there. It will cause damage to his eardrum, and it will become infected. I'll be able to remove it in no time at all under general anaesthetic.'

I had seen Samuel being put under general anaesthetic before, and I didn't want to revisit that experience. The moment he had fallen asleep, there was pure fear in his eyes as he looked at me, not understanding the sensation that had consumed him. The look stayed with me, and I had sobbed uncontrollably until he was woken up. Could I witness that again? No. It was too hard.

'Sammy, please can we try again? Just one more go? Otherwise, you will have to have an operation tomorrow. You don't want an operation, do you? We can get it done now, and then it's all over.' I was babbling. Falling over the words as they quickly tumbled out of my mouth in sheer desperation. 'Please, Sammy. One more try?'

'No. I'm scared.' A tiny voice loaded with insurmountable pain. It was enough.

'OK, love.'

And that was it. We were booked to return the next day, for surgery. What a hideous situation to be in: where your sensory needs lead you towards an operating theatre rather than a simple extraction in a clinic. We had unsuccessfully been in and out of hospital twice already, culminating in being led to theatre, all because of a fear of noises. I can't begin to imagine how that must feel: to choose surgery as a more appealing option rather than two minutes of noise inside the ear.

The next morning, on an operating table, a bead was successfully removed from deep within Samuel's ear. Nobody seemed to know how it got there although I suspected that a little boy may have had more knowledge than he was admitting to. Thirty minutes after surgery, Samuel was back to his usual bouncy self, and I could breathe once again.

Chapter 28

June 2015

After what felt like an eternity of waiting, the day of our urgent CAMHS appointment arrived. The type of urgent that we waited six weeks for. When I made this appointment, I felt like we were close to crisis point. The meltdowns whilst leaving school were daily and becoming increasingly more dangerous. Since then, the transition out of school every day had actually become easier, for whatever reason, but I knew that it was only a matter of time before it all started up again.

Additionally, just because this particular aspect of the day had become easier it didn't mean that life was any more stable. Just a few days earlier, Samuel had tried to cut his face with a pair of scissors. Mia stopped him as the blades were open on his face and was starting to close them together. Mia shouldn't have had to be on hand to stop her brother self-harming. The struggle was still there and just as unpredictable.

Secretly, I was also hoping that the appointment could open doors for me. I was completely unsupported and often felt just as overwhelmed by life as Samuel did because I didn't know how to cope with his behaviour. The day before his CAMHS appointment, I had reached the end of what I could manage on my own. The children were driving me insane. Truly insane. To the point that I was hiding in my bedroom whilst they were screaming and causing mayhem downstairs. I was bored of telling them to be quiet. I was bored of the sound of my own voice. The screaming was relentless and draining, and I had reached the end of my patience.

I felt desperate. What could I do, as a parent, when I had reached the end of my patience? What were my options? I felt like I had tried everything, and nothing had been successful. The only option I wanted to follow through with was to walk out of the door and go for a very, very long walk. On my own. Was that an option?

Samuel had been completely hyper. Like a whirlwind of fizzing energy that never, ever ran out. The trouble was that the energy was contagious. As he spun out of control around the house, gathering momentum, Mia ended up bouncing off his energy, and I was faced with a barrage of uncontrollable hyperactivity.

If nothing else came from our appointment, I had my fingers crossed that there would be something – anything – for me as a struggling, special-needs mum.

The CAMHS building had its usual depressing demeanour as we approached it. I hated this building with all my being, despite its promise of a brighter future for us. Reluctantly, I pressed the entry buzzer by the door.

'Hello, can I help you?'

'I have an appointment at ten o'clock.'

'Push the door and come in.'

As easy as that. No questions about name or who we were seeing? What exactly was the point of the locked door? I pushed it open and entered the gloomy waiting area. We were alone except for the receptionist who was seated behind a glass window.

'Is this Samuel?' she asked. Her expression and voice were warm and welcoming.

'Yes.'

'Hello, Samuel. Do you want to find some toys whilst you wait? There's a toy box over there,' she said, pointing.

Samuel nervously walked over to a table in the corner of the room which had a small box underneath it. In the box was a toddler board book, a small collection of building blocks and a toy car. Pathetic. Was this really the children's wing of the mental health service? Was that the best they could do to help distract nervous children whilst they waited for their appointments? Undeterred, Samuel took the car and pushed it around the floor in silence.

A door swung open and the psychologist walked through, smiling at us.

'This must be Samuel. Would you both like to come with me?' she said, and we got up to follow her. We walked through two sets of locked doors which she released with a card around her neck. *Secure and intimidating.* The room we entered was pleasant enough. It didn't have a clinical feel to it, and the comfy chairs were positioned in the middle of the room in a small circle. A toy box was situated in the corner of the room with a much healthier supply of toys than the waiting room, and there were scales to measure weight and height. The only uncomfortable aspect of the room was that the strip lights felt a little too bright.

Samuel behaved brilliantly for the psychologist. He rolled around the floor, hung off the bars on the windows, climbed under chairs and did just the right amount of screeching. We talked in detail about how much his mental health, and other needs, impacted on his daily life. Talking openly about just how hard he finds every day and explaining meltdowns and instances of self-harm – whilst Samuel listened to every word – was excruciatingly painful He didn't want to hear me talking about any of it, and I didn't particularly like talking about it either.

I found it so hard to answer the relevant questions fired at me by the psychologist which made me feel like my understanding of his condition wasn't adequate.

'Why do you think Samuel feels so anxious every day?' she said.

'I'm not sure. He doesn't cope well with crowds and loud noises, so I suppose the classroom can feel a bit intimidating sometimes. But, he also gets anxious about what people may be thinking or saying about him, and he worries about upsetting people. He also struggles with the transitions in and out of school which gets him very worried.'

I was aware that I had just listed when Samuel became anxious, and not why I thought it happened.

I'd skirted around the subject. How should I know why he gets anxious?

'When did you start to realise that there was something to be concerned about?'

'I'm not sure. Err... when he was a toddler, I think.'

I thought back to how he would always be the loudest in the room at toddler groups, and how I struggled to contain his energy when in quiet situations. Two years old, maybe? It all felt like a blur.

'And what do you think triggers the hyperactivity and makes it worse?'

Oh God, I don't know.

'Lots of noise, maybe? He gets more hyper when there's lots going on around him. If the classroom is busy, with children moving around a lot, it sets him off. But he also gets hyper when there's not enough going on. Like in assembly at school. He can't sit still like the other children.'

I was aware that it was all coming out confused and jumbled. Why couldn't she tell me what was going on, rather than the other way around?

'OK, so what happens once he has become hyperactive at school?'

'He runs around. Jumps on tables. Screams. Leaves the classroom and walks into other classes. Throws things around. Sometimes he even leaves the school building.'

'And how do the teachers manage that behaviour?'

'They don't, really. Nothing tends to work.'

'So, how does he get himself out of it? Or, does it carry on all day once it starts?'

'Sometimes it lasts all day, and I have to deal with

it when I collect him. Other times, he starts shutting down when it all gets too much for him. He takes a blanket into school, and he puts it right over his head until he feels calmer.'

'That's interesting.' She was scribbling away in a pad of paper, listing all of Samuel's faults. It made me feel sad. When I lived in the middle of it, every day, it became normalised. It was just what Samuel did to get through each day. But, listing everything for this stranger felt like a massive breach of his privacy. I was discussing Samuel's most vulnerable moments, to be analysed by the psychologist, without enough consideration of how he must have felt listening to everything being spoken aloud like that.

The questions flowed freely in a torrent of icy-cold waves, and they progressively became more difficult to answer. When the conversation turned to issues of self-harm, I started to feel overwhelmed. I didn't know why he scratched himself or banged his head on walls, and it was too painful to think about in too much detail.

All I could do was to understand that the challenges went deeper than conscious decisions to do harmful things and support him through his daily struggles. I could try to keep him safe. I could give him a loving and safe embrace to retreat to. I could fight his corner every day. I could listen and try to understand.

But, I didn't understand.

'What I'm going to recommend now is to do a full assessment for ADHD. If we can get the ADHD symptoms treated and more under control then hopefully Samuel will be in a better state of mind every day and able to cope with school better. Are you happy with that?'

Was I happy? No, not really. What a question. How could I possibly be happy with my son having ADHD?

'Yes,' I said, feeling deflated.

'There's a questionnaire to be completed. One from you and one from his teacher. They're very in-depth and will give us a very clear understanding of Samuel's difficulties. If the score for the questionnaires are high enough, I will refer you to the psychiatrist to complete the ADHD assessment.'

I sighed. Things were starting to move at last. However, there would be another waiting list to conquer first.

The support, in the meantime, was non-existent. I was left wondering what I would do when he next ran away from school, or when he was smashing his head against a wall in full meltdown, or when he was trying to cut himself. Who would I turn to? Who would help us? What would I do?

However, I left CAMHS with a feeling of relief. Things were moving at last. All we had to do was wait.

*

The dashboard display in my car informed me that it was thirty-one degrees outside. Too hot. I parked up outside school and peeled my clothes away from my sweaty skin as I got out of the car. I was a few minutes early to collect the children, so I slowly ambled around the side of the building, face upturned to the sun, enjoying the warmth as it soaked into my skin.

I heard Samuel before I saw him. High-pitched, ear-piercing screams resonating through the school. My chest tightened, and I hurried to the door. His TA, Mrs Peters, was waiting for me and opened the door, smiling weakly.

'I'm sorry. I think it's the heat. He's just been getting more wound up as the day's gone on,' she said.

'Has anything specific happened to start this?' I asked, watching Samuel climb the apparatus at the side of the hall then throw himself off it, landing heavily on his feet and starting again. I approached him cautiously. If I would have hurried, he'd have run away from me. As it was, he decided to leave the apparatus and walked over to a cupboard where he found a large ball. He kicked it hard and ran after it as it shot across the hall, all the time shrieking loudly.

'What can I do to help?' Mrs Peters asked.

'Could you get Mia, please? And ask her to bring her bag and collect Samuel's things, too?'

'Of course,' she said, and walked off towards the Year 3 classroom.

Alone with Samuel, I tried to talk to him soothingly. 'Have you had a tough day, Sammy?' No answer. 'Do you want a hug?' Samuel stopped for a few seconds and stared at me, as if he was weighing up whether he did want a hug or not, and then carried on chasing the ball. I stood in silence, considering my options. I would either have to wait with Samuel until he felt ready to cooperate and leave the school with me, which could take hours, or prepare to carry him out of school and to my car. This was never an easy decision to make as it was physically demanding carrying him whilst he fought with me, and it made me so upset to do that to him. But, I couldn't really expect school to tolerate me and the two children lingering around, often to a soundtrack of screams, for hours at the end of school.

The door opened and Mia shuffled in, laden down with hers and Samuel's bags. She looked nervous.

'Hello, lovely,' I said. 'You OK?'

'Yes. Is Samuel OK?'

It seemed that we greeted each other like this a little too often.

'He's just a bit worked up. I'm going to get him to the car. Are you happy to bring all of the bags?'

Mia nodded, and drifted further away from me. She didn't want to get caught in the crossfire. I wished I had that option.

Samuel was dragged to the car by myself: kicking, shouting, punching, pinching, biting, trying to push me away, trying to make me lose my balance and desperate to get away from my grasp. I couldn't let him go. He would have run away. It broke me to do that to him, especially with an audience of the rest of the children and their parents leaving school, but what choice did I have? I wished that there was a more humane way to move him in those instances, but I hadn't discovered it yet.

I forced Samuel into the car, but he ran out the opposite door as soon as I let him go. I ran and caught him and tried again. The same thing happened.

'Please, Samuel. We need to go home. Please stay in the car.' I was begging, desperate for him to calm down. I didn't know what else to do.

'Mia, can you get in? Get your seatbelt on. I'm going to have to move quickly.'

The only way I could think to tip the balance in my favour was to play on his anxieties. If he thought I was going to drive off he wouldn't risk running out of the car. He'd be too scared So, with Mia safely strapped in, I turned the engine on.

'The car's running now, Samuel. Don't try and climb out, or the car could move forwards. I don't want you to get hurt.'

I didn't think it would work at first. I pushed Samuel into the back of the car, and he made to run off again. However, something stopped him. The noise and vibration of the car engine scared Samuel enough to make him pause, and I didn't waste a second. Hurrying into the driver's seat, I released the handbrake and edged forwards.

'You need to get your seatbelt on. It's too dangerous without it,' I said.

Samuel screamed at the top of his voice, realising he was defeated, and pulled the seatbelt across his body. The snap of it fastening sent waves of relief flooding through me. I'd done it. The first stage was over. We just had to get home in one piece.

In the car, Samuel threw toys at me whilst I was driving, smacked Mia, stabbed a broken CD case into her leg and drew over the chairs. Mia's desperate voice rose above the chaos as she suffered next to him. I reached my hand back and squeezed her leg.

'I'm sorry, Mia,' I said, feebly. She didn't answer but squeezed my hand back.

We got home, and I opened the car door. Before I could react, Samuel pushed past me, and I watched in horror as he ran off down the road. Mia went to chase him, but I held onto her.

'Leave him. If you chase him, he'll run further,' I said. Leaving him went against all my mother's instincts. I needed to run; to try and catch him; to bring him home in my arms. Instead, with my heart pounding, I watched. Samuel slowed down as he got to the end of our street. He stood there, staring up the road away from our house. *Come on, Samuel. You don't want to keep running. You'll be scared. Come back. Come back to me.* Samuel slowly turned to face me and walked up the hill, kicking stones as he went. I didn't move. I didn't call him or speak to him. I needed to wait for my moment.

And then, after what felt like an eternity of waiting, he was close enough for me to know I could run and catch him. I pounced, and Samuel was squirming under my grip, but I was stronger than him. After a minute or two of wrestling, he was in the house with the doors locked and keys placed up high.

He lost it. All I could do was watch as my house was completely trashed. He threw or broke everything he could get his hands on. Photo frames were smashed, the photos inside them were ripped, chairs upturned, book cases emptied, the television had been pulled off its stand and cups were hurled at me. If I spoke to him, it just fuelled the fire. If I tried to stop him, he attacked me. So, I waited.

I told Mia to keep well away, and she retreated to her bedroom. The floor downstairs was covered in debris, and I could no longer reach him without clearing a path. He was getting tired, though. I could see the fire starting to dwindle, and as he calmed down he got more and more exhausted. Half an hour after returning home, he climbed over the obstacles littering the room and went upstairs without a word.

A few minutes later, I followed and found, much to my surprise, that he had fallen asleep on his bed.

I gently closed his door and went back downstairs, clambered over the furniture and sat in the middle of a house that looked like it had been burgled. I didn't feel anything, just mentally exhausted. I couldn't do this anymore. It was too hard.

Mia quietly came into the room, carefully made her way towards me and we hugged. In silence, we started to clear the room together. The only words that were spoken were by Mia, who said, 'You know he doesn't mean it, Mum? He can't help it. He didn't mean to do this.'

I cried and nodded. 'I know, sweetie.'

*

Samuel didn't wake for hours. Mia had eaten her dinner, had a bath and got ready for bed, and still he didn't wake up. I told Mia it was time for bed.

'But, what about Samuel? He hasn't had any dinner yet,' she said.

'I'll get him something to eat when he wakes up. Don't worry about him. I'll sort it.'

I tucked her into bed and checked on Samuel who was still sound asleep. As I watched his tiny body, free from anguish as his slow breathing made his chest gently rise and fall, my heart broke for him. It wasn't fair. Why should he have to deal with so much pain and confusion at his age? I crept out of the room, with the usual heaviness pulling me down into a dark pit of sadness.

Ten minutes later, Mia came downstairs with Samuel wrapped under one arm. I smiled at them both.

'Samuel's hungry,' Mia said.

'Do you want some dinner, Sammy?' I asked. He nodded without answering. They both sat on the sofa, with Mia holding Samuel close to her own body. He snuggled into her chest and lay there, staring into nothing. I made some cheese on toast for him, and Mia went back off to bed whilst I took over from her on the sofa. Samuel ate in silence whilst I gently stroked his hair, feeling overwhelming pride for my children and marvelling at the courage and compassion they were both capable of which was way beyond their years. I loved being their mum.

Chapter 29

July 2015

The black dog was suffocating me. It had been getting worse all year. Every day felt like a bigger struggle than the last and I didn't know how much more I could take. A black cloud had descended around me and it was growing denser and heavier with alarming speed. I couldn't think clearly. I could barely function. Every day was like wading through treacle. And that was just the physical side.

I couldn't stop crying. Sometimes it was because something had happened. Samuel may have been more hyperactive and louder than usual. Work may have been difficult. I may have been thinking about Robin too much. It was often that. I really missed him.

Sometimes, though, nothing had happened. I wanted to blame my low mood on something, but I knew that there was nothing there. It was a usual day, no more extraordinary than any other, but I was walking around completely separate from the rest of the world as if I was trapped in a little glass box. Isolated. An observer. Not part of society.

I continually felt like I had just had to face the worst bit of news that I could ever mentally process. And I was falling apart. Every day, I crumbled just a little more. It didn't feel like there was anything much left to break now. All that was left were shards of my past life, stinging and sending shooting pains throughout my being with every movement or thought, but even the shards were starting to liquify into nothing. A trail of gloopy, molten glass followed me everywhere I went.

Could anyone else see it? The mess. The cloud. The glass box around me. They didn't seem to. I didn't understand. I looked different. I felt different. Everything was different. Why couldn't they see it?

Why couldn't they see me?

I went to see the GP. Nervously, I waited for my appointment, wondering what I would say. Wishing her to see the glass box, so I didn't need to describe it. Because the words sounded insane. An invisible glass box which followed me everywhere. Encasing me. Separating me from the muted world around. But I didn't think I was insane. I was just melting.

My name came piercing through the speakers making me flinch. Too loud. Too obtrusive. I stood up gingerly, waiting for my glass box to follow. It did. It always did. The doctor smiled as I entered. I tried to smile back, I really did. But it drowned in a flood of tears. Crying and crying, with my head in my hands, grateful for the box around me. Nobody could see me. It was just me.

A hand on my knee. I looked up, and she was in

the box with me. Together. The only person who had ever made it behind the glass walls with me was Robin. But she found a way in. How did she do that?

She talked. I didn't. I can't remember what she said, but time dissolved around us. How long had I been there? Certainly longer than my allocated ten minutes. Eventually, once the tears dried up, she handed me a prescription, and I found my way to my feet. Numbly, walking towards the door, she came with me. Vaguely aware of the queues of people, impatiently waiting for their appointments, we walked straight past them towards the door. A sea of grey faces, void of expression or features, grumbled somewhere in the distance. I was safe from them. We both were. Safe behind glass.

Then she pulled away leaving me alone. Just me and my piece of green paper: a gold-plated pass to normality. Whatever that may be.

Chapter 30

August 2015

After years of waiting, Samuel received his ADHD diagnosis during our first appointment with the psychiatrist. He was eight years old. Four painful, challenging and unfair years of referrals and assessments where Samuel received very little support for his needs, and I had fought until I was sure I had nothing left to give. But, we'd made it.

I didn't feel like celebrating, though. A formal diagnosis was a sickening blow despite the relief it brought, knowing that doors could now open for us. My son had ADHD. A condition which was dripping in pungent doubt and controversy amongst the misinformed and ignorant people who would always surround us. Samuel would have a constant fight on his hands: coping with everyday situations which became too distressing and complex for him and getting people to accept him for who he was.

Before I had even managed to allow the diagnosis

to sink in, I was asked to make difficult decisions regarding his treatment.

'Have you thought about medication?' the psychiatrist asked.

I took a deep breath. I had done nothing but think about medication recently.

'Yes. I've gone around in circles thinking about this for months. I've decided I want Samuel to try the medication.'

Heart racing. Hands clammy. My voice shook. This decision had kept me awake, night after night, as I wondered if I really had it in me to give my son such a strong medication. This was serious stuff. It wasn't wondering whether a Calpol dose was necessary, or whether he'd had too many courses of antibiotics. ADHD medication felt a bit more serious. How would it affect him? Would he stop growing? Would he become a zombie? Would it change his personality? Would it make him feel unwell? Would his eyes glass over with the look of someone taking drugs?

All were genuine fears which haunted me day and night. However, as time passed, my mind started to process thoughts of medication a little differently. Would he be able to concentrate at school better? Would he suddenly start to thrive? Would he be less distressed? Would he be happier? Would all our lives become easier?

Could it be the start of a new life for him? We had to try it.

The psychiatrist smiled. 'I think that's a good decision. Have you read up on the different types of medication?'

Different types? No, I had used all my mental

energy making the simple decision of *yes* or *no* to medication. But, which type? I had no idea.

'I'm not sure. What are the different types?'

'It's the same medicine, but it can be taken in different ways. One of the pills only lasts four hours, so Samuel would have to take it at school, too. If you think that taking a pill at school may be an issue, then we can look at pills which last eight or twelve hours. They release the medicine more slowly into his system. He'll end up having about the same amount of the medicine every day whichever one you decide to go for. The longer release pills come in a few different types. Some release more of the medicine in the morning and less in the afternoon. They can be useful for school if mornings are a problem. Alternatively, other pills release about the same in the morning and the afternoon making it more level throughout the day.'

Woah. My head felt mangled. How would I decide? I looked at Samuel, playing with a car on the floor, and willed some divine intervention to swoop down and take the decision making away from me.

The psychiatrist saw my look of panic and took my hand. 'Take your time. I'll give you an information sheet, and you can go away and read it. I'll phone you in a week, and you can tell me which medication you're going to go with.'

'What if I make the wrong decision?'

'If it doesn't suit him then we change it for a different one. We can be flexible.'

'OK,' I said, nodding slowly, grateful that the immediate pressure was off.

After a week of intensive research, I had made my decision. I decided to go with the twelve-hour pill under the brand name of Concerta. Would it even work? Samuel's anxiety and sensory needs would not be helped by medication. However, I had come to the conclusion that if the medication helped at school and offered him even a ten percent improvement on how he felt there every day, or was able to nudge him one step closer to reaching his full potential, then it was worth trying. Even if it was scary.

*

The day finally arrived. Samuel had been practising swallowing small sweets whole in preparation with mixed success. That morning, though, he was shaking as he took the pill out of my hand.

'I'm really scared,' he said.

'Why, love? You don't need to be scared.'

'I don't think I can swallow it.'

'Yes, you can. You've been practising. You're an expert pill swallower, now.'

Samuel didn't look so sure. The first time he tried he didn't manage to swallow it. Or the second time. Or the third. After many failed attempts, and unforgivable frustration from me, he eventually swallowed it in a spoon of jam. And then I waited.

*

Samuel didn't notice anything different. He said he felt the same as he always did. But I could see it. He played for longer. He was quieter. He sat still. He thought things through. He was calmer. He spoke more quietly. It was fascinating to observe. Finally, I started to relax.

Everything went smoothly until not long after five

o'clock, just as I was dishing up our evening meal. It had been ten hours since he had taken the tablet. Gradually, over the course of the next two hours, I watched him unravel. It was like watching somebody getting drunk, yet it was the complete opposite for him. The drug was wearing off. The ADHD was winning.

Bedtime was challenging for him and me. Suddenly, he couldn't stop. A little firework bouncing off the walls. And he couldn't remember how to sleep. Patiently, I tucked him into bed again and again, taking deep breaths and trying to remember that it had been working. For almost ten hours that day he was winning. He was in control. We still had the challenge of school to face, but for that day, at least, we had a tentative success.

I imagined what people would think of me and the decision to drug my child. The tutting. The judgemental mumblings. Opinions about whether I had taken the easy way out to correct my parenting fails. Would people think that? Or was that all in my head?

Today I drugged my child, I thought. *And no, I don't care who knows. Because, today his future looks a little bit brighter. Aim for the sky, little man, and I'll help you get there.*

PART TWO

Do you see me?

Alone in a paradox of kaleidoscopic darkness
Which consumes me as the colours dance with a
subtle vibrancy.
The only thing I understand is the confusion itself.
I'm lost in an infernal explosion of apathy.

In a mind full of unspoken words, the chaos always
reigns;
Silently screaming to anyone who'll listen.
I'm here. I've always been here.
You just didn't see me;
Enveloped in the shadows, deep within my mind.

Dynamic and free but always restrained.
Imploding energy forever constrained.
An effervescent prisoner locked in an infinite
universe
That boils and bubbles; so hot it could freeze.

I'm fearless, but I'm scared in my transparent cocoon;
I'm trying to escape, but I just don't know how.
The words crash through my mind but dissipate
before emerging;
Lost to you, but not to me.

Open your mind. Look beyond the inferno.
Look deeper. I'm here. The sunshine in the rain.
Silently dreaming. Silently screaming.
I'm here. I've always been here.

Do you see me?

Chapter 31

September 2015

It was my first Cognitive Behaviour Therapy session, or CBT, and I was feeling sick with nerves. It felt like the day I finally admitted that I needed help, and that was so out of character for me. I didn't ask for help. I had never asked for help. Part of who I was consisted of ensuring that I could deal with any crap that was thrown at me. But I wasn't dealing. Inside I was falling apart, but I was also making sure that nobody knew. The daily pretence was exhausting.

In the waiting room, I was convinced that everybody knew why I was there. It felt like I had a sign on my forehead: *Broken Person Hides Here*. But I wasn't hiding anymore. I was there, for everybody to see, in the queue for therapy.

Of course, nobody knew why I was there. I was no different to anybody else waiting for a medical appointment, but logical thinking seemed to have been abandoned as soon I walked through the surgery door. They could all see through my mask and understood me for what I must be. Or so I thought.

And what must I have been? Insane? Unstable? Did needing therapy define me? I was overthinking…

My hands were shaking. My throat was dry. *Calm down.* I couldn't. I couldn't breathe.

'Amelia?' A lady appeared in the doorway. My therapist. My new therapist because I needed mental health support. I flinched before composing myself. Mask on. Smile.

'Yes, that's me. Hi there.' Too smiley. Too loud. She must have seen through it.

'Come on through,' she said, leading the way. Standing up straight, I followed, giving the air of confidence that came with practise when you're crumbling inside.

We talked. Well, Lucy talked. I listened and nodded enthusiastically at all the right places. However, I didn't listen. All my energy and focus were directed towards the act of looking and behaving *normal*.

'How do you feel about being here? Were you nervous?'

Could I lie convincingly? Would a therapist be able to see straight through my pretence?

'A bit.'

Uh oh, the mask was slipping. I could feel it going. Damn, she wasn't supposed to notice. She wasn't supposed to hear the screaming from inside my head. Nobody ever noticed. I could feel it getting louder and louder though, reaching a deafening crescendo. *I'm terrified. I'm terrified of you. Of this. Of me.* I could feel the tears starting to burn behind my eyes. *Not now.*

And, as she talked about the illness called depression, I knew that I wouldn't make it out in one piece.

'It's an illness, like any physical illness. Don't be embarrassed. You wouldn't think twice about seeing a doctor for diabetes, or asthma. This is no different. It's a horrible illness that consumes you and affects everything you do every day. The symptoms have a physical impact on your life making it feel like you're heavy and wading through treacle. I wouldn't wish it on anybody,' Lucy said.

I could hold it in no longer. I wanted to sob. I wanted to enthusiastically nod in agreement and say how awful it felt. I wanted to separate myself from my emotions long enough to be able to speak about how I felt. But instead, I felt myself close in on myself, and a lone tear rolled down my face as I merely nodded.

At the end of the hour I left the room, retreated into the toilets to splash cold water on my face and compose myself. This was me now. Me, with a mental illness. I was sick. And it sucked. Would this now define everything I did? Would all my future decisions, and thoughts, be shrouded with the knowledge that they could be unknowingly influenced by my mental health? And would I know the difference between a rational thought and one that had been suffocated by the black dog? I didn't think I knew who I was anymore, and I didn't think anything would ever feel the same again.

Chapter 32

October 2015

I had been taking antidepressants for six weeks, and I had truly wondered what the point had been. Nothing changed. I still woke up every day feeling helpless and worthless, and the cloud around me didn't even attempt to lift. A sudden good mood was, therefore, unexpected.

It started one day at work. I was in my classroom, talking to one of my students, when a gust of wind outside caught my attention. As the wind noisily whipped around the side of the building, I felt something shift. Something felt different. Having spent months immersed in the deepest, darkest depression, the change in sensation felt alien to me. With every renewed gust of wind outside, I could physically feel the depression lift. I was becoming light. Weightless. As if the wind outside could pick me up and blow me away. And I wanted it to. I really wanted it to.

Thoroughly distracted, I suddenly had an overwhelming urge to be outside. To feel the wind on my face. To have my hair blown away from my neck and feel the bite of the chill in the air. The morning couldn't pass quickly enough as I worked my way around the class, never completely taking my eye off the eerily grey sky outside.

Dismissing the children a few minutes early, I rushed outside, and my body seemed to convulse in a wave of relief. It felt good. I knew the depression had gone. Closing my eyes, I lifted my face to the stormy sky and relished the feel of the wind on my skin. I felt alive. I couldn't remember what alive had felt like before: it had been too long. But this felt good.

At the end of the school day, I drove the short distance to my children's school. The usual heaviness that I experienced whilst driving was replaced by a feeling of floating. The seatbelt was all that was holding me down in the seat. Without it, I could fly.

With the children in the car, I turned up the stereo.

'How has your day been, Mum?' Mia asked.

'Brilliant!' I shouted, over the top of the music. The song changed, and Ed Sheeran's voice danced around the car, exciting me. 'Oh, we must sing to this,' I said, laughing, and broke into full song. The children were delighted and joined in eagerly. I felt good, and I was enjoying the children's company. It was the best.

Arriving at home, I entered the kitchen and – without even thinking about it – opened a bottle of wine. Four o'clock was a perfectly acceptable time for wine. Why shouldn't I?

Things were going to get better, and I was so ready.

*

If I had been skipping when I entered CBT later that week it wouldn't have surprised me. The medication had been working, and I had felt good all week. Really good. So, the response from Lucy wasn't what I expected to hear.

'Are you sleeping OK?' she asked.

'Yes. Well, sort of. I've had lots I want to do after feeling crappy for so long.'

'Yes, that's understandable. So, what kind of things?'

'Cleaning. Tidying. Writing. Oh, I'm halfway through writing a novel.'

Her raised eyebrow surprised me. 'A novel? You haven't mentioned that before.'

'I just started it.'

'And you're halfway through?'

'Yes. Felt really motivated so worked through the night a couple of times.'

Why couldn't I read her expression? I thought she would be pleased. She looked… concerned. I tried to dismiss it.

'So, what's a usual evening looking like? What did you do last night before bed?' Lucy said.

Cautious. What was the right answer?

'I put the children to bed and I cleaned the kitchen.' I hesitated.

'What would that include? Washing up? Wiping down surfaces?'

'Yeah. And the cooker really needed cleaning.'

'Just wiping down?'

Thinking back, I pictured myself with my rubber gloves on, standing on a chair and scrubbing the cooker hood. 'Well, a bit more than that. But it needed doing.'

'What time was that?'

When I started or finished? I must have been cleaning the cooker for well over an hour. 'About eleven o'clock, I think.'

'You were cleaning the cooker at eleven o'clock at night?' Her face said it all. It was the wrong answer.

'It really needed doing. I've just been feeling so crap for so long that I've been neglecting it.'

'I know,' Lucy said, kindly. 'Did you then go to bed.'

'No, I started writing.'

'At eleven o'clock?'

'Yes, about then.'

'What time did you go to bed?'

'About four o'clock.'

'You must be feeling shattered.'

'No,' I said, feeling wary. 'I'm OK. I'm not tired.'

Lucy was concerned. I didn't really understand it. We had spent weeks trying to find ways of making me more motivated and easing me out of the deep pit of despair that I had become so accustomed to. I found a way out. I was happy. I was enthusiastic. At last I felt like I could take on the world. So, why was she so worried?

Lucy said my mood seemed to be overly elevated. I could think of worse things to experience. Depression, for a start. She said that it was probably a consequence of feeling low for so long, and that it would level out in a few days. I didn't care if it did. I liked the way I felt. For the first time in months, I felt happy.

*

My week had been incredible. After my last CBT session, I went home feeling confused but unwilling to embrace Lucy's concerns. I simply felt too good to waste time wondering whether feeling good was a negative consequence of the pills finally working. Surely that concept alone was madness?

Nothing felt wrong at first. So, I had more energy as a result of the depression lifting. That must have been expected, surely? It didn't feel like something I should be wary of. My behaviour was in keeping with somebody who had been held captive for many months, shrouded by depression. Suddenly, I was free.

But, then something didn't feel quite right. Despite not feeling tired, there was a burning behind my eyes, screaming out at me to sleep. How could I sleep, though? There was too much to do.

What happened when the jobs ran dry? When, after a week, the house was spotless and all those annoying jobs that had been niggling away for months were completed, what would I do next? It suddenly became a serious issue. What next?

With the children tying me down to the house my frustration levels started to spiral out of control come the evening. What could I do? Robin's well-timed email asking if I wanted to Skype was a welcome distraction. He still occasionally got in contact, asking how I was. I lived for those moments, however scarce they had become.

'How have you been feeling?'

'Really good. The pills are working wonders. I genuinely feel completely well again.'

He beamed back at me, relief and joy igniting his

whole face. At last! That was the reaction I wanted. This was a good thing to happen. I had to see it as a good thing.

'I'm so pleased. I've been really worried about you,' he said.

And I was pleased, too. Pleased I could finally summon up the energy to talk to him. Pleased with the ease that the words came to me. *I'm back. I got lost for a while, but I'm back.*

Robin carried on smiling through the screen. I tried to relax in his company like I had so many times before. But, this felt different. The screen was just a little too still. Was it the screen, or Robin? Was Robin too still? How could he be? Why wasn't he moving? And he talked so slowly.

Something was building up inside. Frustrated impatience. I couldn't sit there any longer. If Robin wasn't going to move, then I had to. Moving around the house, and taking Robin inside the iPad screen with me, I found more jobs to do. Ironing. Setting the TV recorder. Changing my bedsheets (again). Anything to relieve the pressure that was bubbling away inside. He didn't seem to notice.

Chapter 33

October 2015

The start of the weekend brought half term at school. The children and I were all ridiculously excited to have a week off school. They were especially elated because they were visiting their grandparents for the week in Kent. A holiday by the sea had much appeal.

After delivering the children safely, it dawned on me that I could do anything. Go anywhere. For a whole week I had no responsibilities. The possibilities were endless. For two days I toured around the local shops, but it wasn't giving me the level of stimulation that I craved. I needed something more. So, I walked to the station and got on a train into London. It wasn't planned. I just knew that it was what I had to do.

Part of me regretted the decision as soon as I started walking through Liverpool Street station. The depersonalisation, that depression had led me to experience before, kicked in again as the crowds engulfed me, making me feel like I was watching the scene from a different reality. I wasn't part of their world. Could they see me? How could they? I retreated behind my glass box. I was safe there. Their voices became more muffled as I distanced myself further and further away. But, the more I distanced myself the quicker they all seemed to be walking. Not just quickly, but as if they were following a different time-line to me. Or, like I had been paused whilst they sped past me in fast-forward. I staggered to the wall at the edge of the station and rested my head, relishing the cold feeling against my scalp. Waves of nausea crept up on me and I closed my eyes. *What's wrong with me?*

The feeling passed, and I opened my eyes warily. Everyone had slowed down. Everything looked… normal. With a sigh, I walked towards the underground station with my eyes firmly on the ground in front of me.

I bought impulsive tickets to see a play in the West End. Being able to make quick decisions was exhilarating, and when it ended I bought tickets for a second show. With adrenaline firing through my body, I made my way over to the next theatre and joined the queue to get in. This theatre was much bigger, seating thousands of people. Every sense seemed to be on fire: the smells of the beer and wine clutched in plastic cups as people entered the auditorium collided with the countless different perfumes and body odour as everyone filed past me. The crowd noise was deafening. As the lights dimmed, the rustle of sweet papers made me want to scream. It was uncomfortable and overwhelming; the familiar feeling of tears burning behind my eyes took me by surprise. Why couldn't I cope? It was too much. I needed to get out of there.

The opening bars of music thundered through the auditorium, making me jump, and as the singing started I flinched. Too loud. Too harsh. Then, the applause of thousands of people shattered through my body and I gasped.

Grabbing my bag, I squeezed past the tutting row of audience members to reach the aisle and ran for the exit.

'Are you OK?' A man in a suit was beside me. Official looking and concerned.

'Yes. No. I don't know. I need to get outside.'

He walked me to the exit and I mumbled a thank you before running down the road. *I want to go home.*

*

CBT came around again too quickly.

'How are you doing?' Lucy asked.

'I'm good.'

'Have things levelled out at all?'

'Yes, I just feel normal.'

'Tell me about your week.'

I talked about London. The other things felt unimportant. Who cares if I went shopping, or visited friends, or changed all of the dead batteries that I have been meaning to sort for months?

'That sounds like a nice day out. Had you planned to go into London whilst the children were away?'

'No, but I often go and walk around the shops there.'

'Do you usually go to the theatre, too?'

'No, but I've been meaning to see that play for years.' Suddenly I felt defensive. So what if I saw a play? Thousands do, and they don't have to justify themselves to a therapist. Why shouldn't I?

'If you'd just gone to see the one play, I wouldn't have been concerned, but you went to two. Have you ever gone to see two plays in one day?'

I hesitated. When she said it like that maybe it was a bit odd.

'No, I've never seen two in one day before.'

'And to walk out at the start, after you had paid for the ticket, is very impulsive and out of character for you.'

I didn't answer. Lucy smiled kindly.

'I'm not trying to put a dampener on what you do when the children are away. I'm just trying to establish whether we need to be concerned about your elevated mood, or not. Are you OK talking about this still?'

I nodded and attempted a smile.

'OK, let's move on to the rest of your week. How has your sleep been?' Lucy said.

'It's OK.' A lie. Would she realise?

'So, if we look at last night, for example, did you manage to sleep much?'

I hesitated. Suddenly last night felt like a big deal. A guilty secret. It didn't at the time. But, I knew how it would sound to Lucy. Last night, I had driven to the supermarket at midnight and bought all the reduced meat. When I got home, I decided to cook the larger joints, so I could carve them ready to be frozen. That's normal, right?

But, I forgot the tin foil to cook the joints in. Rather than driving back to the shops at one o'clock,

I decided to wait until the morning. After spending a little more time writing, I went to bed at four o'clock, setting an alarm for six o'clock, so I could go and buy the tin foil. At half-past-six that morning I was cooking.

I didn't tell Lucy.

'I got about five hours' sleep.'

'It's not really ideal. What were you doing?'

'Just writing.'

'OK. Right, well, we need to aim for a cut-off point at ten o'clock. No writing, or housework. You could put music on, or watch a bit of TV, or read until you fall asleep.'

I nodded, only half listening. I wasn't hurting anyone. What did it matter? Lucy seemed to read my expression.

'I don't think the antidepressants are agreeing with you. For some people they are an absolute godsend, but for others they can cause more harm. If there is a hidden mood disorder the antidepressants can uncover it and make your mood overly elevated. Although that could feel nice after being depressed for so long, it's not good if it makes you reckless and take risks.'

I didn't say anything as I tried to translate what Lucy was actually saying. A hidden mood disorder? What did that mean?

'I've brought some questions I'd like you to answer on elevated mood. Are you happy to answer them? It'll give me an idea of whether we need to get an opinion on a mood stabiliser drug instead of the antidepressants.'

What? Mood stabilisers? Aren't they what people in secure

mental health hospitals need to take every day? That's not me.

Yet, I answered quietly, 'OK.'

*

My score was significant enough for Lucy to refer me to a psychiatrist for additional support. I suppose I passed the test. Or failed it, depending on how you look at it. And now I had to see a shrink. How was this happening to me? I walked out of the surgery and straight into the nearest supermarket where I bought the biggest bottle of gin on the shelf. *If I'm insane, I may as well start acting it.*

Chapter 34

November 2015

I thought it would last. It had been so long since I had felt happy, I thought I'd done my time. Everything felt good. For three weeks, I remembered what it was like to be alive. But, it didn't last. Nothing good ever lasts. Along with everything else, my good mood was ripped out from under my feet and left me empty.

No. Not empty. This was worse than empty. Because I had so much more to grieve for. There was depression, helplessness, despair and overwhelming loss for what might have been. I was grieving for my life.

This felt worse than I ever had before. To go from feeling high to crashing down into the depths of despair overnight was more than I could bear. I was craving both the elated mood from the past few weeks and the numbness of depression because all I felt now was pain. A pain I couldn't place. A pain more intense than words could express. And yet, I knew that there was no physical pain there.

If I had a headache, or had cut myself whilst cooking, I would be able to deal with the pain. It had focus and a specific location. This pain, however, had neither. It was everywhere and nowhere. It existed, yet it didn't. It had consumed me, and I didn't know how to ease it.

Nobody could see the pain. They saw me; behaving as I always did. I didn't look any different. No scars. No bandages. No fever. But, I wasn't the same person.

I wanted to ask someone for help. But who? And what help could they give me? They couldn't see this pain. A paracetamol wouldn't take it away. They couldn't do anything. But, I wanted someone to do something. Anything. To notice. To help me. Because I was dying inside, and nobody knew.

I wanted to talk to Robin. I needed him. I had never needed him so much. I needed him to sit with me. To talk to me. To let me cry. To tell me he was there for me. And that he still wanted me. That I was the most important person in the world to him. That I had a purpose. That somebody wanted me. Needed me.

I needed to know that I had a reason to live.

*

The pain didn't ease. It had been a few days, and I still felt it. It was there during everything I did: from the moment I woke up until the moment I collapsed into a drunken slumber on my sofa at night. Robin wasn't there. Nobody was.

I started phoning the Samaritans. I dialled the number so many times, always missing off the last number, then hung up. What would I say? Maybe it didn't matter what I said. Maybe I just needed someone to care. But, I was too scared. Scared to talk to them. Scared to tell someone I had died inside.

I emailed them instead. The message looked so lame: *I can't stop the pain. I don't know what to do.*

Even with just those few, pathetic words, getting the courage to press send was an effort. Then, I waited.

Nobody replied that night. I knew that they wouldn't. The website said to call them if I needed immediate help. It said that emails were not always read and answered immediately. I still hoped, though. I needed somebody to be reading. Surely, somebody would be reading at gone midnight? That's when people like me needed help, right?

I should have called. I knew I should have done. But, my lack of confidence to do so made my mood plummet even lower. I couldn't even manage a call to the Samaritans successfully. A worthless waste of space. Good for nothing.

Angry tears flowed freely, and I allowed myself to sob, gasping for breath after every convulsion. I needed to release the pain which was charging my whole body, but I couldn't define it enough to fight it. Where was it?

I needed to focus the pain. That was the only way to fight it. I had to find it, first. An idea dawned on me, and I immediately stopped crying. What if I could feel the pain on my body?

Without stopping to question myself, I reached in my bedside drawer for a safety pin. Rolling up my left sleeve, I dug the pin into my skin. The sigh of relief was instant. That felt good. In that moment, the mental pain was lost in the aftermath of the sharp prick in my arm. All my body focused on was the newly punctured skin. Digging the pin into my arm again, I then drew it across my skin, leaving a raised, red track from my elbow down to my wrist. Tiny drops of blood eased their way to the surface and smudged the edges of the line.

I stared at my arm in amazement. I didn't intend to do this to myself, but it seemed like the most likely way to help the pain. And it did help. In a weird and troubled way, I felt better. And I slept.

The Samaritans answered my email the following morning. They told me to keep chatting to them. I didn't think I would. I'd found a way to cope, and nobody ever needed to know.

*

At first, I thought that Samuel's medication was working. School had improved considerably, and he was fully integrated back into the classroom. Drop-off and pick-up had been successful every day with no meltdowns or difficult transitions. School had become easy, and I had been sucked into a more relaxed attitude towards his ability to cope. It didn't last.

It had been a slow day at work for me, and I was looking forward to a quiet evening as I walked along the path to the school building. A sound carried through the air and reached me with a crashing blow. Samuel was screaming. Hurrying, I reached the classroom door in time to see Samuel standing on a desk and screaming at full volume whilst the other children sat on the carpet, trying to listen to the teacher. Mortified, and feeling my heart instantly speed up, I opened the classroom door Mrs Peters gave me an apologetic smile.

'How long has he been like this?' I asked.

'He came in from lunchtime unsettled, and it's deteriorated from there.'

Samuel came jumping across the desktops towards me. 'Mummy, Mummy, Mummy, Mummy. Don't listen to them. She's my Mummy.'

I sighed and attempted a smile. 'Hey there, what's the matter?'

Samuel didn't answer but wrapped my coat around him, burying his face.

'Come on, then. Let's go home.'

I felt gutted. This was the first time I had seen this behaviour at school since he had been on the ADHD medication. What had gone wrong? The heavy cloud around me became suffocating as I partly carried him out of the school building and towards the car. I couldn't go back to this every day. Samuel had been coping fine. So, why did he appear to have returned to how he was prior to taking medication? I felt so confused. How can the medication only work certain days?

*

A few days passed, and I received a phone call asking if I could go into school. I was part way through a class when the message arrived, and I looked around me desperately at the children's expectant faces. What should I do?

Another teacher came hurrying in. 'I've got this. You go,' she said.

I hurried my thanks and dashed from the classroom towards my car. What could he have done to need me at school? I called the school office from the car.

'Hi Amelia, thanks for calling us back.'

'What's going on?'

'Mrs Peters has asked if you can come in and help her out. Samuel won't come in from the playground and keeps climbing the back gate wherever anyone goes near him. He's been given distance to try and prevent him from running off although Mrs Peters is watching him. We're obviously concerned, though, in case he falls off the gate or climbs over it.'

My heart sank, and my foot stepped more heavily on the accelerator.

'OK, I'll be there in five minutes.'

The head, Mrs Allan, was waiting for me when I arrived. 'Hi, Amelia. I'm so sorry we called you, but we're worried in case Samuel runs.'

'It's fine. Do you know what started it?'

'No. He just wouldn't come in after PE which finished an hour ago. Mrs Peters is watching him, but we've cleared the area, so he has some space.'

'Thanks,' I said and walked past her towards the playground. Samuel had a ball and was throwing it at the basketball net. He didn't look at me. I walked over slowly and stood by the net. For a few minutes, I said nothing and just allowed my eyes to follow the ball as it hurtled upwards towards the net and then bounced its way back to Samuel. I was intent on not letting him see me as a threat. I needed to get him on side.

After a few minutes of watching him, I moved towards the net ready to catch the ball as it came down. When I caught it, I silently threw it back to Samuel. He caught it and stopped, studying my face.

He then threw it back and nodded towards the net. *It's working.* What a relief. I had him on side.

The silence was interrupted by general activity from close to the school building. The gate had been opened signifying the end of the school day. Mrs Allan was quietly directing parents and pupils away from the playground. I was grateful.

'It's home time, Sammy.'

He looked nervously over to where Mrs Allan was standing, marking our exit from the playground.

'Do you want to get on my back?'

His eyes lit up and he nodded.

'OK, come on then.'

Samuel jumped onto my back, and we silently made our way back towards the school building. Mrs Allan turned around and caught my eye. *Please don't say anything.* I knew that we were on shaky ground, and Samuel could break at any moment. We needed to get home and fast.

Mrs Allan gave me a small, secretive smile and looked away. I breathed a sigh of relief. Samuel had his head buried in my coat, not looking at anyone. I wondered what he must be thinking and whether he was nervous, embarrassed or just drained. Maybe a combination of all three.

Mia was waiting by the exit, holding Samuel's bags. My heart swelled with pride. Such a grown-up girl, having to deal with so much stress every day.

'Is Samuel OK?' Mia asked quietly.

'Yes, he's fine. Thank you for getting his bags.'

'I was really worried.'

'I know, sweetie. He's OK, though.'

Was he OK? Why had he reverted back to struggling this much at school? Every day there were new, complicated problems. He was refusing to do school work, not listening and distancing himself from his class once again. The pills were supposed to help this, but it was no different to how it was before. I didn't understand why. They were supposed to be our lifeline. Now what would we do?

*

I started dreading the walk into school. It was entirely justified. Barely a day went by when Samuel hadn't had some sort of bother or difficulty at school. They looked to me for advice on how to react, but the truth was I just didn't know. Nobody had ever told me. I'd given up asking to be honest. All the CAMHS psychiatrist did was checks his height, weight and blood pressure then prescribe more pills. We didn't just need pills. We needed advice. We needed help. Support. Somebody to tell me what the hell to do when Samuel was throwing things around my house or jumping across the tables in school because I had no idea. Usual discipline techniques fell on deaf ears and made the situation worse. But, what was the alternative?

*

Once again, it was my weekly CBT session. I found it hard to believe that I was so nervous about the sessions when they first started. The fear of the unknown lit the fiery ball of anxiety that constantly resided somewhere deep inside me. Of course, it was unjustified. Lucy had been nothing but supportive and compassionate from the moment she met me.

After a couple of slightly manic sessions over the

previous few weeks, it had felt like a relief to have my old friend depression accompanying me back to CBT. I could breathe more easily without the busy cascade of energy and activity that had engulfed me the previous week. I welcomed the numbness. It felt familiar.

Lucy had given me some activities to complete at my last session based on rethinking negative thoughts. Surprising myself, I had completed the task and had even bought new note books to record my analysis of my thoughts in. Separated into different sections, I had spent time getting my thoughts down on paper and was oddly proud of my achievement. Which sane person felt a sense of pride about writing down their most depressive thoughts? But I did.

I had a blue book for negative thoughts and a red book for more positive moments and memories, and I used a different colour ink for each book. The colours seemed a crucial factor at the time. A strangely significant detail which triggered me to feel a certain way. It was a tiny bit of progress in my desperation to feel well again.

The process was working. As I experienced those moods, I had been so immersed in the negativity that I couldn't see how lost in it all I had become. Writing it down enabled me to distance myself and re-evaluate. It was definitely working. And I wanted to show Lucy. Show her that her efforts were helping. To thank her.

I was ready to tell Lucy how low I had been feeling. It didn't seem to matter because I was trying to improve it. I was engaging in the weekly tasks. So, although I felt like crap as I walked through her door there was an air of hopeful optimism about the session.

Then, Lucy dropped the bombshell, and my hopes of any progress were immediately lost.

'We have a problem with our future sessions. The referral I made to the mental health team, concerning your periods of elevated mood, means that we have to end these sessions. I'm so sorry, I was really hoping that we could carry on, but the referral to a different team changes everything. You shouldn't be seen by two different services. It complicates things.'

Numb. A moment of absolutely nothing inside my head. Empty.

Then the tsunami hit. I wasn't aware that my brain could process so many different thoughts in such a short space of time. Devastation. Abandonment. Anger. Despair. Hopelessness. All at once, they merged together and left my mind screaming. The noise inside my head was deafening.

A burning behind my eyes. *Mustn't cry. Mustn't show my emotion.*

'OK. I understand.'

That's it? That's all I could say?

'I'm so sorry,' Lucy said. 'I suspected it would go this way, and I've been really hoping that your elevated mood wouldn't last. We could have just written it off as a result of feeling low for so long. How long was the elevated mood for?'

'Just three weeks. Nothing too major. It's well and truly gone now.' Desperate.

'It's long enough to be significant, though. I did ask if I could carry on with your sessions, but I've been told not to. It's the right decision. It will complicate things with the psychiatrist if she knows you're already attending therapy. It's the psychiatrist you need to see.' She hesitated. 'Are you OK?'

'Sure. Yes. It's fine. I understand.'

The tears were still there, threatening. I wasn't going to cry, though. And my body was getting heavier and heavier. My mind was getting woollier.

'I really am sorry,' Lucy said.

I was sorry, too. Sorry I screwed up again. I couldn't even do depression right. I managed to mess my life up so spectacularly that I even screwed up my therapy sessions for myself. They were working. I needed it. She said I needed it. The GP described me as 'so unstable' that I needed CBT. Yet, as soon as I could feel it starting to work it got pulled out from under my feet, leaving me reeling. Was I being punished? Was that it? Was it punishment for not behaving the correct way? Should I have hidden the good mood? I thought I was doing things right.

My appointment with the psychiatrist came through for March. Four months away. Four months of nothing. Emptiness. Isolation.

Lucy was the one person who listened to me. The one person who always listened and never expected anything in return. I could selfishly use that hour just for me. As if, for that hour, I was all that mattered.

And then it was gone.

Shit.

Chapter 35

December 2015

I was walking towards school to collect the children one cold but sunny afternoon in December. I felt numb, and I dipped my head to avert my eyes from the other parents. The depression was particularly bad, and it was taking all my effort to put one foot in front of the other and not cry. I wanted the day to just be over. In my own little world, I didn't notice anything different as I approached the school entrance. It didn't even cross my mind that I was the only person approaching the usual gate.

The gate was locked. Looking around in surprise, I saw that everyone was leaving from a different exit. Maybe they couldn't find the gate key. It had happened before. Without a second thought, I walked towards the other entrance. A member of staff was waiting for me.

'Amelia, can you go straight through the playground, please?'

My heart sank. *What now?* As I hurried towards the playground, I turned a corner and saw Mia's worried face.

'Samuel's on the roof,' she said.

'What?' Now running, I threw the door open. Mrs Peters was standing on the far side of the playground with Samuel. He had his feet firmly on the ground. A wave of relief flooded through me as I paced towards them.

'It's OK. We're just talking,' Mrs Peters said. I glanced from her reassuring face to Samuel's lost expression. He looked so small. So vulnerable. My heart broke.

'I think Samuel's ready to go home, now,' Mrs Peters said. I couldn't believe it. She had calmed him down. Not just calmed him down, but enough to get him down from the roof. Another person had successfully managed to do what it normally took me alone to do. I wanted to hug her. *Thank you. Thank you for caring. Thank you for listening to him.*

I held out my hand to Samuel. 'Shall we go home?'

He silently took my hand. I wanted to cry. What on Earth had happened? I mouthed the words 'thank you' to Mrs Peters and set off across the playground.

*

It was my final CBT session. I almost cancelled it: after all, what was the point when the therapy had been ripped from under my feet so unceremoniously? A big part of me wanted to stick two fingers up at the system and scream loudly at them.

'So, you think you can break me? You're going to deny me my therapy before I get better? Well, guess what? I'm leaving you first. This is my choice. Not yours. I'm the bigger person, here.'

I knew that was ridiculous. Their plan wasn't to break me. It was purely a ridiculous paperwork issue. The CBT only covered depression. For us special cases we had to wait for special therapy sessions organised by special doctors – at some point during the next year.

The decision still hurt.

I arrived at the GP surgery and took my usual seat in the waiting area, waiting for my turn to be called. Lucy appeared almost immediately, smiling warmly.

'Hi, there. Come on in,' she said. Her smile didn't quite reach her eyes, and she had an air of unease. Maybe she also thought that ending my sessions so abruptly was cruel and heartless. It wasn't her fault.

I got up a little too quickly, trying to show that being rejected for further sessions hadn't bothered me. I was OK with this. Honestly, I was.

I wasn't, though, and I wondered if Lucy could see through my act.

'How has your week been?' Lucy asked.

'Oh, it's been fine.' I couldn't say anything more. I couldn't lie, and I couldn't tell the truth, either. *Since you rejected me last week, I have cried and felt worthless and a failure pretty much every day,* I thought. She didn't need to know that.

'I'm so sorry we have had to cancel these sessions. You do understand, don't you? You will be treated much better by the community mental health team and can start therapy again through them.'

But my initial assessment appointment's three months away. Three months! Why can't we carry on until then? This was helping, damn it. It's so unfair.

However, I said, 'Yes, I understand.' It was easier

to agree. There was no point in me demonstrating my emotional response to the rejection. There was no point in anything. What I thought didn't matter.

Three months felt like a very, very long time away.

Lucy opened up a page on her computer screen. 'Here, move closer so that you can see. As it's your last session, we're going to write a *Staying Well Plan* together. We'll look at what the triggers are for the depression and elevated mood, so you can see it coming. Let's start with the depression. If you were to feel it coming on now, what would it feel like?'

This is stupid. Staying well? But, I'm not well. And I had been immersed in the darkest depression for a couple of weeks, so what would the point be in analysing the trigger? I wasn't trying to hide from depression, or sneakily divert away from it when I saw it coming. I was trying to escape it. I was the depression. Why couldn't she see that?

*

I walked out of the surgery feeling hopeless and let down. Nothing that was discussed during the last hour would help me fight my depression. I could feel myself dropping lower and lower, yet I had just wasted an hour of my life being told how to spot myself falling. Too late. I'd fallen. And I didn't know how to get back up. Maybe I never would.

The rain fell heavily; an echo of my desperate mood. It was all downhill from there. I lifted my face to the cold downpour and relished the spiky feeling on my skin. Sometimes it was things like that which grounded me and made me remember that I was part of this world. Too often, I just felt like a spectator: observing how connected other people appeared to be. So vibrant. I watched on from behind the glass. Isolated. Empty. Void of life.

Maybe my life wasn't worth the same as theirs. Maybe my life had been segregated for a reason. Maybe I wasn't meant to be there.

*

The phone rang. I groaned as I looked at the caller ID. School.

Not again. Not today, I thought.

I didn't answer. I didn't have the strength to. This was their time. For six hours a day, I didn't have to do it. Someone else could. I fought for the best part of a year to get full-time 1:1 support for Samuel because he needed that extra bit of help. That wasn't me. Not that time. They would have to deal with him until the end of school. Not me.

The phone fell silent and I waited. How long before the voicemail kicked in?

Bzzz.

That wasn't long. That meant it was too serious for them to explain in a voicemail. They wanted me to call them back. Or go in.

I didn't listen to the voicemail. It was all too much.

*

I waited outside Samuel's classroom door and my heart was racing. Maybe I should have called them back. What would they say to me?

Mrs Peters was waiting for me and left the classroom. I felt sick.

'Hi, we've been trying to get hold of you this afternoon. Did you get our message?'

'No, sorry, I haven't looked at my phone yet. I've

come straight from work.'

I noticed her swift glance down to my jeans and pumps – it was obvious I hadn't been teaching – and she forced a smile. 'Samuel isn't feeling well. He has a stomach ache and has been feeling sick. He's a bit hot, too.'

Just when I thought I couldn't get any lower, a curveball smacked me in the face and I sank deeper. There was a ringing in my ears and everything around me faded into the distance. The glass wall around me became denser, and a feeling of smog engulfed me. I couldn't hear her talking anymore. It was like a magnet had drawn me down towards the ground, pulling at everything, making my skin drag downwards. Walking was slow and an effort. Samuel was sitting at his desk, looking flushed and sleepy. Somehow, I made it over to him, wading through guilt and self-hatred.

'Hey, Sammy. Not feeling too good?'

Samuel didn't answer but buried his face in his rhino. My heart ached.

'Come on then, sweetie. Let's get you home.'

'Can you carry me?'

Could I? I could barely carry my own weight in that moment.

'Of course I can. Up you get.'

Mia was suddenly behind me, looking concerned.

'Is Samuel OK?' she asked.

'He's just got a bug. Can you take his things for me, please?'

Mia knew the drill too well. She always ended up taking Samuel's things, whilst I carried him out of school. Only, that day was different. He wasn't shut down. He was sick.

And I didn't go and get him until the end of the day.

The guilt was too much. I could feel tears prickling behind my eyes, and I buried my face in Samuel's shoulder as I lifted him up. He smelt funny, like I could smell the bug that was consuming him. We walked through the crowds of parents outside the classroom door, and I could feel them all staring. Usually I felt so invisible, but today they stared. And they knew. They knew that I had left my sick child at school whilst I wallowed in self-pity at home.

I hated myself. With all my heart, I hated everything about me.

Chapter 36

December 2015

Late again. Samuel wouldn't put his socks on that morning, which resulted in me screaming at the top of my voice again. It never worked. I don't know why I did it. In fact, it had the opposite effect. Samuel hated the screaming and went into himself even more, blocking out all external input. So, why couldn't I stop myself from doing it?

I was tired. I didn't want to scream. I didn't want any of this. I knew I needed to be a better mother. I felt it inside. I felt compassion towards his needs. I had understanding. Yet, I just couldn't stop myself. It was almost a habit. Samuel refused to do something, I shouted, he still didn't do it, I shouted some more, and then I hated myself for not showing that I understood him better. Then we were late. We were always late.

As I hurried into my school, I got a sympathetic smile from Jane on reception.

'It's OK, Amelia. Breathe. Sarah's started the class for you. She said to take as long as you need, and she'll get them reading until you're ready.'

I smiled gratefully at Jane.

'Thanks. It was a difficult morning. I'm surprised I'm here at all, to be honest.'

Damn tears. They threatened to escape as I opened up to Jane. I managed to control myself, but she knew. Maybe it was the blotchy red face I always got when I was about to cry. Or the waver in my voice. She stood up and hugged me. It was the worst thing she could do: the hug acted as a pressure release to my emotions, and a fat tear trickled down my cheek.

'I'm sorry. I normally contain myself better. So stupid.'

'Don't be daft. Nobody expects you to contain it. None of us know just how hard it must be to look after twins on your own. Especially considering Samuel's needs. Go and get a cup of tea, and I'll tell Sarah you'll be in shortly.'

I smiled gratefully and wiped my eyes. 'Thanks, Jane,' I managed to say although my voice cracked, and I headed towards the staff room.

The staff room was empty. I put the kettle on and made tea, taking deep breaths to compose myself. Sitting down in a chair, which wasn't quite comfortable enough and forced me to sit upright, I wondered if I could get away with listening to my Headspace app for ten minutes. I would feel a right prat if anyone walked in to find me meditating, but I had an overwhelming urge to close my eyes and get lost in my breathing.

I made my tea, put my headphones on and

searched for the depression pack on the app. I was supposed to listen to it every day to get the full benefit, but I always forgot. Or I was too busy. Or too lost.

The familiar voice was like an old friend. My breathing immediately slowed down, and I quickly immersed myself in my own bubble of calm.

*

Sarah smiled warmly as I entered the classroom, twelve minutes later. Just enough time to meditate and down my cup of tea. It warmed me from the inside, and I felt ready to face the world. Ready to face anything. Actually, I felt good.

The class were sitting in silence whilst Sarah held up an A4 worksheet. Gradually, all the children looked up and smiled as they saw me. They were pleased to see me. I felt something fizzing inside.

'Has everyone got a worksheet? Excellent. Read the two texts in silence, and then we'll discuss them.'

I quietly walked towards Sarah, and she squeezed my hand. 'You doing OK?' she whispered.

'Yeah. Thank you. You're an absolute star, you know that?'

'Any time. I wasn't sure what you had planned for this class, but I found these worksheets in the cupboard. Hope you don't mind.'

'No, not at all. I'm just grateful. Thank you so much.'

Sarah squeezed my hand again and quietly slipped out of the classroom. I looked around at the calm, bent heads and waited – slightly impatiently – for them all to finish. Something inside me was keen to get started.

'Have we all finished?'

A quiet murmur rippled around the room. They hadn't finished.

Come on.

I took a board pen and turned to write the date on the board. Suddenly feeling creative, I made the letters fancy, allowing the pen to swirl and curve as it formed the words and numbers. Oblivious of the children behind me, I rubbed the numbers out – dissatisfied with the way they looked – and wrote them again. Stepping back, I cocked my head to one side and admired my work.

'Very pretty,' a voice from behind me said. It wasn't an unkind voice. She meant it. A warm buzz inside my stomach fluttered excitedly. I turned to face them.

'Thanks. So, have we all finished now?'

They nodded and the general murmur this time sounded more positive.

'Let's make this fun. Everyone who has an answer will get the chance to write it on the board. There will be a prize for the best, most creative answer, and a prize for the best, most creative handwriting.'

The students were smiling and there was a buzz of excitement in the room as they talked to each other.

'OK, settle down,' I said.

'What prize, Miss?' a boy called Josh asked.

'I have a Kit Kat in my bag. Two fingers for the best answer, two fingers for the best handwriting. Will that do?' I could feel myself getting excited. This was a good idea. This would engage the students. I was a good teacher. The best teacher.

'Right. Two texts. Two authors. Who can tell me something about the authors?'

Almost every hand shot up. I grinned inanely. 'We're keen today! OK. Jake?'

Jake looked pleased with himself. He wasn't usually this keen to answer a question. He suffered with confidence issues and worried too much that his answer may be wrong, and how silly he would look in front of his peers. Not today, though. He knew the answer, and he had a determined look of courage etched across his face. I was pleased I'd asked him. I was giving him this moment.

'The second author usually writes horror stories,' Jake said.

'Good. Name one.'

'It.'

The answer was predictable. I expected he hadn't read *It*, but famous books were generally known by students thanks to the films that followed. I wanted to ask him for a second book by the same author but stopped myself. This was Jake's moment. Don't blow it.

'Brilliant answer, Jake. Come and write it down.'

Jake went red but looked proud as he scraped his chair back and nervously walked to the front of the class. I handed him the pen. He wrote simply, with no swirling letter formation. I was disappointed, but I didn't show it.

'Thanks, Jake. Can anyone name any other books which Stephen King wrote?'

Five hands shot up. Four girls and a boy. The boy, Alex, was an avid reader. I would probably need him to answer more in-depth questions later, so I turned to the nearest girl.

'Maisie?'

'Carrie. I'm reading it at the moment.'

'Great! Not for the faint hearted, that book. Come and write it down.'

Maisie glided to the front of the class with the air of a ballerina and took the pen. She squinted her eyes with a look of concentration, and the pen swirled beautifully as it flowed across the board.

Inside, I was bouncing. Inside, I was bubbling. I was enjoying myself.

'What about the other author? What did he famously write?'

One hand went up. Alex. I threw him my best, beaming smile.

'Yes, Alex?'

'Of Mice and Men,' he answered and came to write it down. Alex was sensible and wrote it in his usual handwriting, and again I felt disappointed that my brilliant idea hadn't been embraced by all the children. Looking around the classroom, I spotted the students who were more likely to play the game. The trouble was, they were not necessarily the most active readers in the class. I needed a question that they were likely to be able to answer.

'What is the common theme? What are they both writing about?'

It was a simple question. They were writing about writing. *It's that simple. Come on*, I thought. But, only a couple of hands went up. I picked a girl who was more likely to be flamboyant, and she came to the board. She didn't disappoint, and her fluid movements twisted and glided as she formed the letters. I clapped my hands excitedly.

'Brilliant! Well done. Next question: there are other comparisons within the texts, or common themes. Name another one, please.'

Again, I chose my student carefully, as I decided which were more likely to play the game.

'Jack?'

Jack was one of the cool boys. He didn't even answer first but swaggered to the front and took the pen. With very large, graffiti style letters, he wrote the word *DESKS*. I clapped again.

'Exactly. They're writing about the furniture they use to help them write.'

The urge came from nowhere. As Jack handed the pen back to me, I threw it in the air, twirled around, caught it and held it like a microphone.

'Right. Who's next? I'm looking for a difference in the style of writing between the two texts.' Still using the pen as a microphone, I put on my best, deepest, voice-over voice. 'Will it be Pippa who stuns the audience and answers next? Or Ethan? Who will be the winner of today's Kit Kat? You decide.' The students were laughing. They thought I was hilarious.

I was winning at life.

*

When I collected Mia and Samuel from school, I linked my arms through theirs and we skipped to the car. Mia was laughing.

'You're in a good mood today,' she said.

'I know. Let's make the most of it. How about we go out for dinner tonight? Who fancies pizza?'

They cheered, and I put my arms around their shoulders to squeeze them tightly.

'Come on, then.'

There was a lightness to my body. The usual heavy drag of depression had lifted; I felt like I could float. Getting in the car, everything felt different. Usually, as I drove, I felt my heaviest. Depression sucked me down into my seat, pulling on my facial features, making my face long and expressionless. Moving was an effort. But, today? If the seatbelt wasn't securing me to the seat, I believed I could float away. I pulled forward in the seat, closer to the steering wheel, and fiddled with my phone in search of rock music. Bon Jovi thudded through the speakers at full volume.

'You have to sing for your supper, kids,' I said, and they joined in enthusiastically.

*

At the Italian restaurant, I told the children to order whatever they wanted. They looked surprised.

'Really? Anything?' Mia asked.

'Sure,' I said. 'Whatever you like.'

I wasn't hungry, but I ordered a pepperoni pizza. I could always take it home. The waitress asked about drinks, and I turned to the back page of the menu. I felt like celebrating. Celebrating not bringing the black dog with me for once. I didn't know why he had run off, but I wasn't complaining. I felt amazing.

'Can I have a glass of champagne, please?'

The children stared at me, open mouthed, but said nothing. The waitress smiled and walked away. As soon as she was out of earshot, Mia turned to me.

'Champagne?' Mia asked.

'Sure. Am I not allowed a glass of champagne?'

'You're driving,' she said. 'And you always say it costs a fortune.'

'Well, thankfully I just asked for a glass and not a whole bottle, then,' I snapped. She was sucking my good mood away. How dare she? I worked bloody hard and had to put up with daily crap, at home and at school, plus I'd been secretly fighting depression. Why the hell shouldn't I have a glass of champagne?

The food arrived, and I picked at my pizza, only really eating one slice. The champagne was divine: ice-cold and gloriously bubbly. It effortlessly slid down my throat, like liquid silk, and I shuddered with pleasure. But, it was gone too quickly. Impatiently, I stared at the children's plates. Samuel and Mia had barely started their pizzas. I wasn't sure if I could sit still there, waiting for them, for much longer.

'Eat up,' I said.

'I'm full,' Samuel said. He had hardly touched his pizza. Bloody medication, stealing his appetite.

'OK, leave it. How about you, Mia?'

'I'm *not* full. I'm going to eat it all,' she said. I sighed; I could swear she was eating in slow motion.

An idea started to form in my mind. And I started to wonder why I had never thought of it before. I could write a song. After all, I played piano, and I was an English teacher. Poetry couldn't be very different to song lyrics. How hard could it be?

Half listening to the children talking about their days, I started to construct some ideas for lyrics, carefully weaving the lines together until they made sense and flowed beautifully. It was a song about being happy. No more crap about being depressed, and certainly not a love song. I didn't need love to be happy.

Silently, I internally sang a few ideas for a melody. The first couple of ideas weren't good. But the third one was amazing. Really, really good. I hurried off to the toilets and sang it into the video camera on my phone, so I didn't forget it. Listening back, it sounded good. I could do this.

*

Back at home, I cleared the piles of paperwork which always found their way onto the electric piano, and I plugged in my headphones. *This song won't write itself*, I thought, and I started experimenting with chord sequences alongside my lyrics. It felt too easy. Completely engrossed, I was oblivious to Samuel and Mia staring at the television for an hour. Two hours. Three…

Oh God, bedtime.

'Kids, it's bedtime.' They didn't move. 'Come on, it's time for bed.'

'After this finishes,' Mia said.

'No, Mia. It's late. Now.'

Samuel screamed. I felt my temper bubbling.

'That's enough,' I shouted. 'Bedtime. Now.'

Mia got up, but Samuel pulled his blanket over his head, refusing to move.

'I will only read a story to you if you are ready for bed by the time I count to fifty. OK?'

Samuel screamed again, but this time he ran upstairs. I felt smug. I'd got this parenting thing sorted.

I rushed the bedtime routine, but thankfully they were so tired that they didn't seem to mind too much.

A quick story, four short songs and I pressed play on Samuel's MP3 player. Gentle piano music drifted daintily through the air, and I kissed him goodnight.

'Love you, Mia. Love you, Sammy.'

'Love you,' they both said.

'Can you sit outside my room until I'm asleep, please?' Samuel said.

The same question every night. He didn't need to ask. I always sat outside their room. I loved to know that he felt safe. Secure. I wouldn't dream of not sitting outside his room.

'Yes. Nighty nighty, sleepy tighty.'

I sat outside their room, humming my new song. Irritatingly, it clashed with Samuel's music, so I stopped. Resting my head on the cool wall, my eyes closed wearily.

Something changed. There was a fog, oozing its way towards me through a barren valley, and its heavy darkness started to engulf me. Familiar, yet unwanted; I slipped deeper and deeper into its murky depths.

Why? Why now?

The black dog was back.

Chapter 37

December 2015

There was an email waiting in my inbox from Robin. Just two simple words.

How goes?

How would I answer? An hour before, I had felt like I could take on the world. Then, suddenly, the waves of depression were surging towards me and gaining momentum with each thunderous crash. The undercurrent was more than I could handle, and it pulled me lower and lower until I knew that I would drown. I was defenceless and didn't know how to fight it, so I succumbed to its power.

I ignored Robin's email. There were no words to explain how I was. But why? Why did I have such a good day, and then this? Suddenly, Lucy's face popped into my mind. What would she say?

Elevated mood.

It was part of all the crap. That wasn't me being in

a good mood. It was the bloody illness screwing with my head. Making me happy.

What had changed? What was so different? Why were my changes of mood so extreme? My mood elevated for just twelve hours before the crash. Feeling manic was new to me. It had felt so normal at the time, but looking back, I was mortified and embarrassed.

Could it be the antidepressants? If the elevated mood was not due to the antidepressants working, then could it be that the antidepressants were making me sicker? I reached for my phone and Googled elevated mood and antidepressants. The first result was an article about mood swings with antidepressants.

I needed to talk to someone. Reaching for my phone, I called Robin's number.

'This is a nice surprise,' he said. 'Are you OK?'

'Yes. I mean, no. I don't know.'

A moment of silence, then Robin answered, 'Tell me what's going on.'

'Have you ever realised that I was depressed without me telling you?'

'Yes.' His answer was too quick, and I was taken aback.

'Really?'

'Yes. I can tell just by the tone of your emails when you're feeling depressed.'

Wow.

'OK, so how would you describe my mood when I'm not depressed.'

I could hear Robin smiling down the phone.

'Happy. Care-free. Positive.'

I took a deep breath and stole myself for the next answer. 'Would you ever have described me as manic?'

His answer was just as quick as the one before. 'No. Definitely not.' There was another pause. 'Why do you ask? What's happened?'

'I was manic today.' My voice was quiet and almost unrecognisable. I was embarrassed.

'Right. OK. Are you sure?'

'Yes, I'm sure.'

'What happened? What did you do?'

'I felt different. Light and bubbly. I played stupid games with my students and made a tit out of myself. I took the kids out to dinner, and I drank champagne instead of eating.' My voice dropped to almost a whisper before admitting the last part. 'And I wrote a song.'

'Well, that is all rather out of character. How are you feeling now?'

'Depressed.' My voice cracked, and a tear rolled down my face. 'I think my antidepressants are poisoning me.'

'Why would you think that?' His voice sounded stern. Not what I was expecting.

'Because the elevated moods have got worse since taking them.'

'Have you researched the medication? Is that a side-effect?'

'Yes, it is. Antidepressants can make the mood swing from low to high.'

'But, millions of people take antidepressants. They

203

can't all be manic. Why do you think it's affected you that way?'

'I don't know. Maybe they just don't agree with me.'

'Remind me why you have to see a psychiatrist? What was the therapist's reasoning?'

I flinched. I didn't want to see a psychiatrist, and I wasn't enjoying talking about my mental health like this.

'Because my mood is swinging high and low, I've been told that a mood stabiliser may be needed.'

'Can that be taken instead of the antidepressant? Will it make you steadier and less swingy?'

'I think so. I'm not sure.'

'When's your psychiatrist appointment?'

'March.'

'No. That's too long. You can't wait four months. Not if you think the medication you're taking now is causing you too many side-effects. Look into a private psych. I'll pay.'

'I can't take your money,' I said.

'And I can't sit back and do nothing when you're sick and it could be eased by a different drug. I won't take no for an answer.'

I didn't tell him the real reason why I disliked taking his money. Sometimes, a hug would solve everything and accepting money instead made me feel uncomfortable. I could have his money, but I couldn't have him. It felt like a replacement and made me a bit sad.

However, I knew that he was right. I couldn't afford a private appointment and waiting until March could be disastrous.

'OK. Thank you,' I said, quietly.

'It's nothing to worry about, love. I've known you for years, and you've been nothing but steady. We just need to stabilise your brain chemistry, and you'll be back to how you used to be. It's just an illness. We'll sort this.'

I didn't answer. It didn't feel like an illness. I was being poisoned by the antidepressants. Maybe the psychiatrist would understand that.

*

Sitting in the GP's waiting room, clutching printouts of local psychiatrists, I was reminded of doing the same for Samuel last year. Back then, I had nervously waited to see the GP, expecting a fight on my hands to get a referral to CAMHS. There had been no fight as it was obvious that Samuel was in need of mental health support. But, it was now my turn. And I hated it. I didn't want to need mental health support. I was partly hoping that the GP would refuse the referral for me. I wondered if he would tell me that my need was not great enough to need an immediate, private referral, and to simply wait for the appointment in March.

My hands were shaking. Why was I so nervous?

Dr Rimmer came to the waiting room rather than calling my name over the speakers. Did he not trust me to go in on my own?

'Miss May. Please do come through,' he said.

I tried to smile, but it was a feeble attempt, and I followed him through to his room.

'How are things? Is your medication working OK for you?'

He hadn't read my notes. Lucy had explained on there how the medication wasn't working and had referred me to the community mental health team. I really didn't want to have to explain all of this to him.

'No, it's not really working,' I said. Internally, I was screaming to him, *Please read my notes.*

'I can increase the dose for you. That's no problem. You're only on the middle dose for it at the moment.'

He started typing away on his computer. I had to stop him. I had to explain.

'No. I can't go on a higher dose. The CBT therapist said it isn't advisable.'

'Ah, OK. Give me a minute, I did see that she had written something down here,' and he started to read. My heart was pounding.

'Right. That makes sense. You're waiting for an appointment to discuss mood stabilisers. Have you heard anything from the community mental health team yet?'

'Yes. I have an appointment in March.'

'That's a long wait.'

'I know. That's why I'm here. I've researched a few private psychiatrists. Do you think it's worth getting a referral to see one a bit sooner?' I could feel myself nervously rushing to get the words out. I braced for the answer.

'Definitely,' he answered, a little too quickly. My heart sank. 'If you're able to pay for it, then I think this needs to be sorted as soon as possible. I'm just sorry that the NHS wait is too long.'

He thought I was an urgent case. He thought I

206

couldn't wait. I certainly didn't feel any relief at his words.

'I can do the referral at lunchtime and fax it straight over to him,' he said.

'Thank you.'

'Until then, you should stay on the medication at the same dose. The psychiatrist will then advise you about how to safely change from one medication to another. Does that sound OK?'

'Yes.' It didn't sound OK, but I had no energy to explain so accepted the prescription.

'Make an appointment with me after you've seen the psychiatrist.'

'OK. Thank you.' Why did I feel so vulnerable as I answered him? Like a child being told by an adult to do something that scared them. All of this scared me.

'I'll see you soon, then,' he said, and I nodded as I got up to leave.

*

It had only been a few hours since I had seen Dr Rimmer, and my phone rang. The number was a local one, but I didn't recognise it. Tentatively, I answered.

'Hello?'

'Hello. Is this Miss May?'

'Yes.'

'It's Doctor Wright. I'm a consultant psychiatrist from Aldwich Consultancy. Is this a good time to talk?'

I hesitated. I didn't feel ready for this.

'Yes, it's OK.'

'I received a referral today from Doctor Rimmer. I actually have an appointment free tomorrow evening at 7pm. Would that be a good time for you?'

Tomorrow? Oh God. I needed to sort childcare. And I needed to prepare. Could I do that by tomorrow?

'Yes, tomorrow's OK.'

Inside, I was screaming. I had to be ready.

'Great. Would you mind giving me your email address, please? I can send you the clinic details and patient agreement to sign before you get here tomorrow.'

I read it out to him, concentrating on keeping my voice steady. I wondered if he could sense how scared I was? He must have been able to. He was a psychiatrist, after all. They're mind readers, right?

'Great, thank you. I'll send the information out to you straight away, and I look forward to seeing you tomorrow evening,' he said.

'I look forward to it. See you tomorrow.'

*

Another day, another appointment. But, this was the scariest one so far. Luckily, my neighbour had agreed to babysit, but this also filled me with panic. What if Samuel played up? What if he refused to go to bed? I really hoped I didn't go home and find her traumatised whilst Samuel was playing indoor football. It was possible. Anything's possible with Samuel.

I was a stranger to those streets. It was dark, there seemed to be a shortage in street lights, and, according to the clinic notes, the building I needed did not have a big sign outside it: to protect patients' privacy. I tried to remember from the email what the front of the building looked like, but the row of terraced Victorian town houses all looked identical.

I noticed that none of the houses appeared to be

residential homes anymore, and most of them had signs distinguishing which business operated from there. I used this to my advantage: surely the building I needed must be the only one without a sign? I kept walking up the hill and came to a gate with no sign attached. I pushed the gate forwards and approached the front door, more than a little concerned that I could be walking up to someone's front door to their home. However, by the door-bell there was a small badge which read Aldwich Consultancy. Thank God.

I rang the bell and the door was immediately answered.

'Hello. Miss May?'

'Yes.'

'I'm Doctor Wright. Well done for finding us. Please, follow me.'

I was taken aback by the speed he answered the door. He was waiting for me. I was expecting to get a few minutes in a waiting room, to collect my thoughts before going in, but I was immediately led into an attractive sitting room with large, comfortable-looking armchairs. I was surprised as I looked around. It wasn't like any other doctor's room I had seen. It wasn't clinical, and it felt homely although the ambience of the room did nothing to ease my nerves.

He sensed my panic. 'There's nothing to be worried about today. We're just going to chat about how things have been. I'll ask some questions, make some notes and see if I can suggest anything extra that may help you. Does that sound OK?'

'Yes. Thank you.' My voice was shaking.

'Why do *you* think you're here today?'

'Because my antidepressants are making me manic.'

Doctor Wright smiled kindly but didn't comment on my statement.

'Why don't we start from the beginning? Tell me about when you started to take the antidepressants.'

It was like the flood-gates had been opened. I told him everything. I couldn't stop myself. I told him about my awful year with Robin, and how depressed I had become. He asked if I had been depressed before that, and I explained how the first time was after the twins were born.

'Did you seek help then?' he asked.

'No. I thought it was just baby blues. At first, I couldn't bond properly with the twins. I remember wondering how I would feel if someone were to take them away. I didn't know what the answer to that would be. I didn't feel like their mother. I couldn't admit that to anyone, so I didn't say a word. And then, my husband died when they were still babies. Everyone expected me to be low.'

He nodded sympathetically, writing everything down in his notepad, and then asked me about other times when I had felt depressed. I found that I could talk about it for the first time ever, like he had given me permission to let go.

'Do you ever think about hurting yourself?'

This wasn't the first time I had been asked this. Every time I saw a GP, or therapist, they would ask me. I usually lied. Something inside urged me to be honest this time.

'Sometimes the mental pain I feel inside is too much. I can't make it feel better. So, I scratch myself to distract from the hidden pain. It's a relief to focus on actual pain rather than the pain of the depression.'

I couldn't look at him.

'Is it ever more than just a scratch?'

'Sometimes,' I whispered.

'Do you ever think about ending your life?'

Outside, through the window, I could see a group of women laughing. I wondered where they were going. To a pub? Theatre? Cinema? They looked so happy. I couldn't remember the last time I had done anything like that.

'I think about ways to end my life. But, it's complicated. I couldn't ever do that to my children. So, I think of ways to make it look like an accident. They can't blame me, then. They'd be sad, but they'd get over it. I had a cut on my finger, by my nail. It was feeling really sore, and then it became quite hot to touch and a bit swollen. I thought it was probably infected. I should have made a doctor's appointment for antibiotics, but I decided to leave it. I was hoping it would turn septic.'

I stopped talking and stared at my finger with interest.

His voice was without judgement, and he didn't sound shocked. 'That's not a great place to be, though, is it?'

'No.' I still couldn't look at him. 'I fully understood the risk, too. I knew that sepsis could kill me quickly. Nobody would find me in time. There's nobody who would check on me.'

He was writing. I glanced over at him. He was calm and genuinely looked like he heard this sort of talk every day. He didn't look like he was about to section me.

'What about elevated mood? Have you experienced

that before?' he said.

Strangely, I felt more nervous about discussing this than suicidal thoughts. I had to pick my words carefully.

'Not before taking the antidepressants. They made my mood elevated.'

'Your doctor says that the therapist suspected hypomania. Why do you think she said this?'

'Because the medication made me do odd things.'

'What did it make you do?'

I squirmed uncomfortably. 'I became very impulsive and had lots of energy. I wasn't sleeping much.'

'Did you spend more money than you usually would?'

I thought back to the new speakers dotted around my house. 'Yes.'

'What about alcohol? Did you drink more, at unusual times?'

'Yes. Sometimes. I drank champagne straight after school one day.'

'Have you been in trouble with the police?'

'No. Definitely not.'

'And, how about your driving? Has it been more erratic?'

I remembered how I jumped a red light, too impatient to wait for it to change. 'No. My driving hasn't been affected.' Some things he didn't need to know.

'What about any big ideas that you're able to do something that you wouldn't normally consider doing?'

'No.' But, I remembered the song writing. Did I really want to tell him that?'

'You just thought of something, didn't you?' he asked. How did he do that?

'OK, there was one day...' I stopped, too embarrassed to go on.

'It's OK. You can tell me anything without being judged. I can assure you that I have heard it all before. What happened?'

'I thought I could write a song. It became a bit obsessive, and I thought it was really good.'

'And was it?'

I smiled nervously. 'No. It was dreadful.'

He smiled kindly. 'When did you realise it wasn't good?

'Later that night. As soon as I felt my mood drop.'

'It dropped the same night?'

'Yes.'

'How long had it been elevated for?'

'Twelve hours.'

He didn't answer but started writing. I wondered what he was thinking. Surely, what I had said was enough to make him believe that the medication was wrong for me. I just needed him to believe.

It was feeling like an age since he had last spoken, but he eventually looked up from his papers.

'I think it's obvious that the current medication isn't working for you. Would you agree?'

'Yes, definitely. It's sending my mood too high.' I felt relieved. He understood.

'I don't think it's the medication doing that. Although antidepressants can cause episodes of mania, or hypomania, we usually find that it's a difficult job to get the mood to come back down. Your mood, however, is up and down. I don't think that is entirely the medication. What we need to do now is to stabilise your mood, to stop it swinging from low to high, and try to lift the depression that you're currently experiencing. Your current medication isn't helping that on its own. What I suggest is introducing a mood stabiliser. Now, don't be put off by this, but the medication I think would suit you best is actually an antipsychotic. In higher doses it's used to treat schizophrenia. However, you will take a much lower dose which will act as a good mood stabiliser. It will help to stop it swinging back and forth so much. How do you feel about that?'

He looked at me expectantly. I felt my jaw open, as if to speak, but nothing came out. This was too much. Information overload.

Schizophrenia?

Not the antidepressant?

Antipsychotics?

No words came.

'I know this is a lot to take in, but it will make you feel better and that's the most important thing here. The medication is commonly used to treat mixed moods including depression.'

Numb.

I stared out of the window and tried to process what he has just said. Gradually, I managed to bring my attention back to the doctor. He looked like he understood. I tried to smile.

'How do you feel about trying the mood stabiliser?' he asked.

How did I feel? I felt like I didn't have a choice. This was what I had gone there for, after all.

'OK. I'll try it.' Was that voice even mine?

'Good. I'll write to your GP to recommend he prescribes the new medication.'

Again, he was writing. My head was a mess. I couldn't process everything he had said. After a minute or so, he looked up and smiled.

'Doctor Rimmer will have the letter by lunchtime tomorrow. You can then contact him for your prescription.'

And that was it. We were done. He was showing me out of the building, shaking my hand, and he'd gone. I stood in the dark street and closed my eyes.

What just happened?

Chapter 38

December 2015

It felt unfair that life went on as if nothing abnormal had happened whatsoever. The night before, I was told that I needed to take an antipsychotic drug. The next day, life carried on as if nothing had changed. My appointment almost felt like a dream. Except, I knew it wasn't. And I had some big decisions to make.

I decided to call in sick at work. I needed time to think about everything that had been said at the appointment. School was understanding – although I told them that I had a sickness bug, which bought me forty-eight hours off – and I returned home after dropping Mia and Samuel at their school.

Going back to bed, which was where I felt the most relaxed and calm, I grabbed my iPad and started searching for information on antipsychotics. I still couldn't get my head around it all. I wasn't psychotic. I was sent to the psychiatrist to get a mood stabiliser, not an antipsychotic. Why would he do that?

I read page after page of information about the new medication. My head was spinning. I closed my iPad and started pacing. There must have been some mistake. The usual feeling of tears prickling behind my eyes was there, and I gave in, allowing them to flow freely. What happened to me? How did I end up visiting psychiatrists and popping antipsychotics?

I needed to know more, and I couldn't read whilst crying like a baby. *Get a grip. I have to get a grip.*

Taking a deep breath, and wiping my eyes, I turned my iPad on again. What's the new drug like? I read through the side effects. Not too scary. No different, really, to the antidepressant I had been taking. Sedating. Weight gain. *Brilliant.* As if I needed more of that. But it was no great shock.

I knew I should have stopped there. I knew I shouldn't delve into the dark side of google, but I couldn't help it.

What does the drug feel like, once you've taken it?

I read. And I cried. Painful sobs which wracked my whole body, constricting my chest and making my head hurt. I wished someone could hold me. I needed someone to hold me. I didn't want to do this anymore. I didn't want to be me anymore.

Don't expect to be able to wake up.
You will have no mental capabilities.
Driving is a challenge.
You may need to cease working.
Looking after children is not advisable.
It is, basically, a human tranquiliser…

At some point I think I must have cried myself to sleep. The alarm on my phone disorientated me. Had I slept all day and night? Oh my god. The children.

Grabbing my phone to turn the alarm off, I could see that it was my three o'clock reminder to collect the children from school. It was fine. It was still daytime. Looking in the mirror, my eyes were still swollen. I didn't have time to put makeup on, so I splashed my face with cold water before heading out to the car.

My mind had calmed down, and I had some resemblance of clarity. I wasn't going to take the new medication. And I was going to stop taking the antidepressants. That was what started all of this. I didn't need them. More than that: I would be better off without them.

Starting now. I am a drug-free zone.

And, for once, I felt good.

*

The snow fell overnight, sending the children into a premature Christmas whirlwind of excitement and hyperactivity. The snow-coated images on the front of the dozens of Christmas cards dotted around the house now seemed to make sense, and there was a general buzz of festive cheer everywhere I turned.

I could see it. And I understood it. But I didn't feel it. I was back behind my glass window of apathy. The world could do one. I wasn't interested. It was more than that, too. The pain was excruciating. With every breath, every heartbeat, every blink of the eye, my soul splintered a little more. Razor-sharp fragments of my past-self broke off into tiny crystals and glistened into an ever-growing stream in my wake. All the bright and sparkly parts of me were gone, destined to be just a memory.

The children wanted me to build a snowman. They couldn't see the river of my soul, shimmering behind me and growing larger with every passing second as I was bled dry. So, I built a snowman. The icy-cold snow was a shock to my senses. It was something I could feel. I relished the sensation and removed my gloves. It was almost painful, and a relief to experience something other than the mental pain which had consumed me.

'Mum, let's put the head on now,' Mia said.

'No. It needs to be bigger,' I said, scooping more snow onto the body. My movements were slow. Deliberate.

'Like this?' Samuel asked, thrusting snow hard into its side. A cascade of snow fell as a result. I flinched.

'That's too hard. Slow down a bit. You'll break him,' I said.

Samuel laughed and threw another large pile into its side.

Don't spoil it. Don't spoil my snowman, I thought. Why was this so important? What did it matter? I needed the snowman to not collapse. I had to finish him. It was important that I finished him. I didn't understand why.

Samuel was the first to get bored and ran off to make snow angels on the ground. Mia quickly joined him. I was relieved. I didn't want to talk to them. I wasn't cross. I wasn't anything. I just couldn't talk.

*

The twins' school had managed to remain open, despite the snow, but my school was closed due to not enough teachers being able to get in. After much disgruntled complaining from both children they got to school, only a few minutes late. I could never do anything on-time anymore. My body and mind were on permanent go-slow.

I couldn't quite explain how I was feeling. The depression had sunk to an all-time low. Plus, the withdrawal from the antidepressant was awful. My stomach hurt, and I felt sick. But, it was nothing compared to what the pills were doing to me.

I didn't want to go home, so I put my snow boots on and went for a walk into town. I didn't have any money with me, but that was OK as I wasn't shopping. I just needed to walk. The sun was trying to burn through the mist, but it wasn't strong enough. It was like me. Stuck. Peeping out, but not quite connecting with the world. I stopped and stared up into the sky just as the sun became completely obliterated by the clouds and mist. My heart sank. That's what I had to look forward to. Isolation and elimination.

Because there was nothing left.

And, in that moment, I knew. I didn't want it anymore. That was the point when I said enough was enough. Nobody was around to realise. Or care. It was just me. The way it always was.

Suddenly, things seemed clearer. I knew what I needed to do. I needed to disappear, quietly and without a fuss. No more fighting. No more pretending everything was OK. No more pain. Just... nothing.

I started walking again towards the ring-road. The ice on the footpaths made them treacherous in places. It was like it was meant to be. Just one slip. One well timed slip. That's all it would take. Nobody would be able to prove it wasn't an accident.

The traffic was slower than usual. Damn. Although some drivers weren't slowing down for the icy conditions. I just had to pick my moment. Pick my car. Or lorry. There were quite a lot of lorries driving along there. They wouldn't be able to swerve quickly or stop in time.

Here. Here's a good spot.
Yes. Here.

*

I was so close to the curb. When I closed my eyes, I felt the whoosh of the lorries as they passed. I felt it through my whole body. A warning of how close I was. Ironically, this was the most serene and sane I had felt in a long time. The first time I had been completely sure of myself. Everything seemed to make sense. This was the moment I had been working towards. I kept my eyes closed and concentrated on my breathing. Slow and deliberate, each breath took me one step closer to where I needed to be. Free of pain.

Occasionally, a car horn threatened to pull me away from my breathing. Why were they beeping me? I wasn't hurting anyone. It was just me and my bubble. And I was waiting. Waiting for the exact moment when it felt right. The exact moment when my breathing had transported me to the next stage. The stage when I felt ready to slip. I knew that I was close, but I wasn't quite there yet, so my focus returned to my breathing.

In, two, three, four, five, six, seven, eight.
Out, two, three four, five, six, seven, eight.
In, two, three, four, five, six, seven, eight.

Out, two, three four, five, six, seven, eight…

I was ready.

'Amelia?'

No!

'Amelia, how long have you been here? You're freezing. I was driving past and saw you. What are you doing?'

Leave me. Please, leave me.

'I've parked my car just around the corner over there. Come on, and I'll take you home. Amelia?'

My neighbour, Ellie. Why was she there?

'Brrr, it's pretty cold out today, isn't it? I'm wishing I'd put a hat on,' she said.

I was ready. I could still be ready, if she left me.

'Your hands are red raw. How long have you been out here?'

My eyes remained closed. I returned to my breathing. I could get back to where I was.

In, two, three, four, five, six, seven, eight.

Out, two, three four, five…

'Are the children back in school today? They must have loved the snow. I saw their snowman in your garden. It's brilliant.'

She didn't realise that I made it. It was my snowman.

'I imagine they'll be making more at school today. It's all so magical for them. Especially just before Christmas.'

Oh God. My children.

Images of my children flooded my thoughts. Their smiling faces that morning. Their laughing. Their twinkling eyes and mischievous grins. The way they hugged me before bed. Who would hug them tonight?

I knew I couldn't do it. *Not today.*

'Come on, Amelia. Let's go home.'

I opened my eyes and allowed Ellie to guide me away from the road. I didn't cry. I didn't speak. There was nothing left to think or feel. In that moment, the racing thoughts were silenced.

'Would you like to come back to my house?' Ellie asked.

I knew she was concerned, but I didn't want to go to her house. I wanted my bed.

'No, thank you. I'm not feeling well. I just want to go home.'

Ellie nodded and pulled the car onto her drive.

'Shall I pop over later?' she said.

'No. I'm fine. But, thank you for the lift.'

'OK.' She sounded unsure. I didn't care. I didn't want to think about her. I didn't want to think anymore.

I wished everything could just disappear. Like the snow. One moment it was there, the next...

Chapter 39

December 2015

The alarm woke me in time for school. I was disappointed. Disappointed that I was still there. Shit.

The children were arguing. It was the first sound, after my alarm, that welcomed me to my day. Why couldn't they stop fighting? Every morning was the same. I was sick of it. Sick of everything.

A niggling thought had been squirming its way towards me through the fog. I needed the drugs. I really wasn't OK without them. I would rather be manic than this. And maybe, just maybe, I needed to consider the antipsychotic, too.

I took my antidepressant. It felt like admitting defeat: I didn't want to be taking medication. I didn't want to feel suicidal, though. It was so hard to explain, but although I didn't want to die it seemed like the only realistic outcome. The only way to ease the pain. If drugs were the only way to improve my outlook on life, even marginally, then I had to give them a try. If only for my children's sake.

Without even commenting on the children's bickering, I ordered Mia and Samuel into the car. I drove in silence, thankful that there appeared to have been a truce on the backseat.

Samuel didn't want to go in to school. He hugged me and clung on desperately, quietly pleading with me to stay. It was another wake-up call. He bloody needed me. However crap a mother I was at that moment, he needed me. I *had* to get well.

Samuel was peeled off my leg by his teacher, and I ran to my car. All of a sudden, I had a level of urgency that I hadn't felt in a while. The suicidal ideation was still rattling around my head, but now there was a counterattack which needed addressing quickly. I needed to find an alternative to death. It had to be out there, somewhere. If it's at the bottom of a pot of antipsychotics, then who the hell was I to reject it? I owed it to my children.

I had a free period first thing and wasn't teaching until ten o'clock. I would normally sit in the staff room and make sure my lesson plans were OK for the day, and photocopy any resources that I might need. However, I thought that sorting out my mental health was a far better use of my free time.

My usual pharmacist was in my local supermarket. I walked past the counter a few times, pretending to be shopping, whilst I waited for there to be nobody else around. At last, it was empty, and I approached nervously.

'Can I help you?' He didn't look like the pharmacist. Maybe he was a general member of staff.

'Is the pharmacist about, please?'

'Sure, I'll just get him.'

My hands were sweaty, and my heart was beating too fast. Tears were threatening. *Mustn't cry. Not now.*

'Hello, can I help you?'

He was older and more professional looking. The other, younger man was still lurking. I didn't want an audience.

'Is there somewhere I can talk to you confidentially, please?' I asked. My voice was shaky and little more than a whisper.

'Of course. We have a room just here.'

I followed him in, trying to keep control of myself, and took a seat opposite him at a desk. But, now it felt so formal. I could feel my confidence sliding away. *No. I'm stronger than this. Just ask him.*

'I've been prescribed some medication for mood swings.' I passed him the psychiatrist's letter with the drug recommendations printed on the top page. He took the letter and read.

'Ah, yes. It's a good medication.'

'Is it really? Because I'm really scared about it.' The tears flowed too easily. 'I've been reading about it, and it sounds horrific. It says that I will feel like I've been tranquillised, and I won't have any mental capabilities and will sleep all day, and I shouldn't drive or look after the children. I can't be like that. I'm a teacher, and a mum of two children. But I can't stay like this, either. Every day I just wish for my life to end…' And I was sobbing. Sobbing for the life I'd lost. Sobbing for the mother I should be. Sobbing out of pure fear.

The pharmacist took my hand. I was grateful for the human act; so many people were scared of human contact, but that hand across the desk was enough to slow my cries. Enough to allow me a second to breathe. Enough to show me that I wasn't alone. Human contact. Something I never received anymore, from anyone except my children. It wasn't enough to heal, but it was enough to matter. Like a plaster, or a bowl of chicken soup.

'There really is nothing to worry about,' he said.

'Really?' I couldn't hide the surprise from my voice.

'Yes, really,' he answered, warmly. 'It's a low starting dose, and the gradual increase will mean that your body will adjust easily. Maybe take a few days off work, until you're sure that you've got used to it. Don't plan anything that you will need too much mental ability for. After a few days, you'll be fine. I have lots of people I prescribe this to, and none of them are zombies. They have jobs, and families, and drive cars. You'll be fine.'

'Oh my god, seriously?' I asked, hardly daring to trust the relief that was seeping into my mind.

'Yes, of course.'

'But, all of the stuff online?'

'Never believe everything you read about medication online. Yes, some people react badly to some medication, but they are in the minority. It's like, if you read reviews for holidays online: the people who had a great holiday never go online to write a review. However, the people who had a bad experience are straight on there, telling the world about what happened to them. But, they're a minority. The same applies to this.'

'Yes. That makes sense,' I said.

'And the overriding factor here, is that the doctor

would not have prescribed this for you unless he thought that the benefits would outweigh the side-effects. It's a very good drug, and you *will* feel better on it.'

I wanted to hug him. He had given me hope. Something I never thought I would ever have again.

I left the consultation room and walked straight to the spirits aisle, picking up a bottle of gin. I thought I might as well get pissed that night before I started the new medication. After the week I'd had, some gin therapy was undoubtedly needed.

*

They were staring at me from across the table. The strong, silent type. So small, but they knew they had the upper hand. They knew that they were going to win this standoff. No matter how hard I tried to fight it, I would undoubtedly end up surrendering to their persuasive powers.

It was such a tiny pill. But that pill had floored people in the forbidden, online world.

Just take the damn pill.

I can't.

I got up and started distracting myself. Washing up. Sorted school bags. Polished school shoes. But, all the time, I could see them staring at me. Waiting. Taunting me.

'OK, you win,' I said. To the pills. *I'm talking to pills now.*

It was so small. The smallest pill I had ever seen. Yet, it had the power to turn my world upside down. Or, the right way up. Maybe inside out for the first few days. I wouldn't know until I took it.

Just take it.

'I'm scared.'

Nobody answered. There was nobody there. There was no option, really, other than to get a grip and swallow it. Nobody was going to either talk me into or out of this. This was something I just had to do.

Maybe... maybe... what if I take just half a pill? That sounds less scary. I can do that – what's the worst it can do? Then, tomorrow, when I feel a bit braver, I will take the whole thing. Yes. That's what I'll do.

I found my pill cutter and carefully cut it into two halves. Placing one half in a pill container, I swallowed the other one before I could change my mind. *That's it. Done.*

*

I couldn't feel anything. It had been an hour, and I couldn't feel anything. Maybe I should have taken the whole pill. It hadn't affected me in the slightest. All that panic, for nothing.

*

Lying in bed, I put a film on my iPad. This was the worst part of my day, every single day. The time when I would have once sat with Robin on Skype, until I fell asleep. He would stay with me until I slept, and then he would go to bed. Losing that crutch was the hardest thing of all. I didn't want to fall asleep alone. So, I put a film on to try and distract me. Sometimes it worked. Other times, I couldn't see the screen through the tears.

The film had only just started, but something wasn't right. The screen wasn't quite in focus. And my head. Wow, my head – it was spinning. Like I'd had far too much to drink, and the walls wouldn't keep still. I felt sick. *I should get up. Get some water. My eyes, I can't keep them open... I can't...*

*

My phone was ringing. I couldn't open my eyes. I couldn't move. I didn't know if it was night or morning. It stopped ringing.

*

The alarm shocked me into consciousness. Tentatively, I opened my eyes. How did I feel? Groggy. Very, very groggy. But, I was awake. And I could sit up. OK, that wasn't too bad. I was awake and sitting up. It could be worse. But, I really needed a shower and a cup of tea.

I stood up, and the walls rushed away from me. My stomach lurched, and I stumbled back on to the bed. I wasn't expecting that. Bloody hell, I felt awful. Closing my eyes, I very gingerly rested my head back onto the pillow. *Just five more minutes. I don't need a shower.*

Five minutes stretched into fifteen minutes. I had to do this. I had to get up. The children were ready for school, but I hadn't made packed lunches, yet. *OK. Do it. Get up.*

Everything felt slow. Laboured. Painful. And, I couldn't think properly. My head felt... empty.

*

Driving actually felt like my brain hurt. The children were delivered to school safely. *Now, just me.*

Walking into school, I felt sick. Diverting into the toilets, I slid down onto the floor and rested my head. The cool wall was welcoming. I couldn't teach. I couldn't even talk. Why couldn't I talk? My words were too slow, like I'd forgotten how to form the letters in my mouth. I'd just give the kids reading to do.

230

By the time I had reached morning break, I started to feel more human again. I only took half a pill the night before. I was supposed to take double that, and repeat it in the morning, and then double it again that night. I couldn't do it. I just couldn't do it.

*

I found myself in the same place again, later that day, staring at the pills. This time, as they stared at me, they weren't just taunting. They had an evil glint in their eye and they laughed maliciously, knowing full well what lay in store for those who dared. Did I dare? I had no choice. I couldn't stop and start psychiatric medication – that would really mess with my head.

So, the big question was: half a pill or the whole thing?

Sod it. The whole pill. Kill or cure. In that moment, I didn't care either way.

I didn't feel sick as I put that night's film on. My head wasn't spinning. But, I was tired. I didn't think I could watch much of it. *I'll just rest my eyes for a second.*

*

The drive was hard work again. But, I took half a pill before I left for school, and I was coping. Albeit slowly, but I was coping.

*

The GP, Dr Rimmer, only gave me five days' worth of the new medication. I guessed he wanted to check I was tolerating it. Was I coping? I thought so. I had taken my medication that morning, and I was only half a zombie. Although I was regretting a nine o'clock doctor's appointment. There was no way I was going to be able to pretend I wasn't off my face at that time. Maybe that didn't matter. Maybe that was what he was expecting.

Dr Rimmer came to the waiting room to get me. I liked the gesture. It was so much friendlier than being called over the speakers.

'Hello, there. Come on through,' he said. I followed, wondering whether I looked drunk when I walked.

'Day five, then? How are you getting on?' he asked.

I swallowed. It was hard to swallow as my mouth was so dry. Another side effect, I assumed. My mouth opened to speak, but I couldn't quite remember which words I needed.

'I'm... OK.'

'How are the side effects?'

Swallow. 'Improving.' Swallow. 'I think.'

'And are you coping on it? Driving OK?'

'I just need to... concentrate a bit more.' I really was finding it hard to talk. 'I find... when I'm talking... I can't... always remember the words.'

I felt stupid.

'That will ease. It's early days, and you're just adjusting to the medication. What about those racing thoughts of yours? Is your head any calmer?'

'It's quiet. My head... it feels quiet.'

'That's the medicine working. Well, it seems like you're doing really well. I'll give you enough for another month, then come back and see me again. Does that sound OK?'

I was doing well? He thought I was doing well.

'OK. Thank you,' I said.

I was doing OK.

Chapter 40

January 2016

It had been a month since I started the new medication, and I had acclimated well. It no longer made me feel tired, I could speak with normal ease and my brain didn't feel foggy. Most significantly, I no longer had hyper, manic mood swings. However, the low mood was proving a little more difficult to shift. Every day, I wallowed in the usual pool of soul-sucking depression.

And then, things suddenly got worse. A lot worse. I found myself in a dark place where nobody cared enough to support me anymore. CBT had stopped, the GP didn't want to see me every week anymore and I was still waiting for the appointment with the community mental health team. I was well and truly on my own.

Unable to control the depression, I found myself in a deteriorating whirlpool of unhelpful thoughts and hopelessness. And I couldn't shake it off. The mental pain was so intense, I didn't know how to function anymore. Something had to happen.

And it did. One evening, after the twins had gone to bed, I sat and cried as the low mood shrouded me. I didn't know where the thought came from. Was I even thinking? Maybe it was a subconscious action with no level of rational thought involved. I walked into the kitchen and took a steak knife out of the drawer. The knife hadn't ever been used and had a sharp, serrated edge to the blade. I let it rest on my arm, soothed by the cold, prickly feeling of it against my skin and stayed still for a few minutes, enjoying the relief I was unexpectedly starting to experience.

Then I applied pressure and pushed it hard into my skin. Slowly, so slowly, and maintaining the pressure, I dragged the blade across my inner arm. I gasped with relief as I felt the depressive feelings ease slightly. How did that work? The sting was intense, and the pain lingered, minutes after the knife had stopped sawing through my skin, leaving a deep red, slightly raised line across my arm. And, as I stared at the line, the distraction was enough to take the memory of the mental pain away. It didn't last long, but it had been the only relief I had felt in months. For a short while, I felt better.

That was the turning point in my life. My self-harming had stepped up a gear. Sticking a safety pin into my skin no longer offered a workable solution to my depression, but the knife was working. Every day, I sliced another cut into my arm, which I kept carefully concealed under long sleeves. Nobody knew. Until that fateful day.

Chapter 41

April 2016

The children were at school, but I had called in sick. My mood was so low, I couldn't imagine how I would be able to communicate with anyone enough to teach. I'd been phoning in sick a little too often; how long before I was called in for a chat about my absences? I didn't care, however. I was too sick to work.

I sat in a very quiet house, and my mood sank lower and lower. I didn't help myself: I had looked through old photos of me and Robin and found a video of us together. It was a weird situation how whenever I felt low I made myself desperately sad by thinking of Robin. Why couldn't I stop doing things which triggered my depression?

Closing my laptop, a little too harshly, and wiping my eyes, I decided to run a bath. A bit of pamper time could be just what I needed. I dropped a bath bomb into the running water and the room became a steamy, rose-scented sanctuary. Taking a deep breath, and feeling my heart slow down, I stepped into the hot, pink water, trying to clear my mind.

My mind, however, was not to be cleared. As each minute passed, I was sucked deeper and deeper into the fog as the sadness consumed me. There was no reason for it. There were no specific thoughts plaguing my troubled mind. I just felt desperately sad.

I cried. Every breath in and out became a loud sob as I gave in to the waves of hysteria. Unable to comfort myself, I scratched at my face and chest, trying to inflict pain. It wasn't enough. I needed proper pain. And blood. And to give my body a violent shakeup.

My razor was right next to me. Digging my nails into the plastic by the blades, I tried to rip it apart. My nails gave way first. Looking around me, I grabbed my tweezers and tried to use them on the plastic, gauging the thin edge into the join of the plastic. It worked. The razor popped apart, and the four blades were exposed.

I didn't even think. Taking a blade, I drew it once across my wrist, not too deep. With intrigue, I watched how easily the blood flowed. Much more easily than with the knife. Balls of blood oozed to the surface, and when I lowered my arm into the water it dissipated, leaving the cut clean. I put the blade against the same cut and drew it through the skin again, this time with a little more pressure. There was more blood this time, and I gasped with relief. More. I needed to do more.

Again, and again, harder every time, and the depression eased momentarily with each cut. Then, as suddenly as I started, I knew that it was enough.

Slowly, placing the blade down, I lowered my arm again, rinsing the blood off into the water. Bloody streaks stretched out into the bath in long, swirling ribbons, turning the water a deep crimson colour. I studied it in fascination. Calm. Serene. Healed.

Except, I wasn't healed. My mind may have felt relieved in that moment, but the blood flowed persistently from my wrist, and it dawned on me that it wasn't going to stop. Pushing down on my wrist with the palm of my hand, I tried to ease the flow with pressure. Five minutes. Ten minutes. It didn't show any signs of stopping.

Oh God. What do I do?

Wrapping the hand towel around my arm, I carefully got out of the bath. Keeping the towel in place with my body, I used my other hand to dry myself and put some clothes on, feeling the rising panic growing stronger every second. Where should I go? Doctors? Accident and Emergency? Minor injuries? Or, phone for an ambulance?

I sat on my bed, my mind struggling to process any thoughts whilst immersed in the depressive fog. I had plasters and bandages in my bedside cabinet from previous self-harming incidences, and I took a bandage. Removing the towel, I winced from the pain which was starting to become uncomfortable as the initial relief subsided. The blood flow had slowed down, and I wrapped the bandage around my wrist with great difficulty. It wasn't a great first aid job, but it would do. I decided to head to the minor injuries department at the local hospital as the bleeding looked like it was getting under control.

Driving was difficult. I felt very protective of my

left arm and found changing gear a painful challenge. By the time I reached the hospital, my heart was pounding, and I felt in a state of shock. What had I done?

The receptionist called me forward and took my personal details. She typed ferociously, her fingers speeding across the keyboard. I stared at them, dreamlike, in a state of shock.

'What's the injury?' she asked.

'I've cut my wrist.' My voice shook and was little more than a whisper.

'Left or right?'

'Left.'

'How did it happen?'

I said nothing. I couldn't. I just stared at the wall behind the receptionist's desk. She paused from her typing and looked up at me, kindly. Understanding dawned on her.

'OK, Amelia. Take a seat. The nurse will see you soon.'

I shuffled away and sat down, choosing a seat far away from everyone. I wanted to dissolve into the fabric of the chair, invisible from everyone's judgmental gaze.

'Amelia?'

A nurse had appeared next to me, and she smiled warmly. I got up and followed her into the triage room, my heart pounding so powerfully she must have been able to see it. She gestured to a seat next to hers, and I sat down in silence.

'How did this happen, Amelia?'

Pause. 'I did it.'

'Can you tell me why?' Her voice was calm. She didn't sound like she was judging me.

'I was so sad.' Tears started to well in my eyes. 'I have depression. I was just so sad.'

She passed me a tissue and rested a hand gently on my knee. 'Come on through. Let's get you sorted out.'

I followed. A lost lamb, struggling to fend for myself. She led me towards a chair and disappeared for a minute, returning with a small, silver tray containing dressings and sterile cleaning solution. She talked whilst she wiped the blood off my wrist.

'Are you under care of the crisis team?'

'No.'

'How long have you been self-harming for?'

'I'm not sure. A few months, maybe.'

'Who knows about this?'

'Nobody,' I whispered. There was silence for a moment, whilst she applied butterfly stitches to my cuts and then deftly wrapped a bandage around the wound.

'I need to contact the mental health team. Somebody will come here to see you. I also need to call social services, so I need some details from you about your children.'

My mind exploded, and panic flared through me. *Social services?*

She read my expression correctly. 'It's nothing to worry about. You're not in trouble. We always contact them for mental health issues when there are children involved. They will just see if they can do anything extra to support you. Don't panic.'

I nodded feebly. One moment of self-destructive

madness and my situation had suddenly escalated beyond what I had ever thought possible to happen in my life. The nurse disappeared to make the calls which would turn my world upside down, and I waited, aware of just how vulnerable I had become.

Chapter 42

Two Years Later, July 2018

The alarm woke me, and I quickly silenced it. It was early. Very early. Crawling out of my sleeping bag, and succumbing to the huge yawn which escaped me, I reached over towards where the twins lay. They hadn't stirred from the alarm and were still breathing slowly, snuggled deep inside their sleeping bags. I smiled. Their faces seemed to always make me smile these days. Especially as they slept.

'Sleepy heads. Wake up,' I whispered, gently shaking them. Rubbing their eyes, they quietly sat up.

'What time is it?' asked Mia.

'Four o'clock,' I answered. 'No more talking, or we'll upset the other campers if we wake them up. Jumpers and shoes on.'

We all pulled warm jumpers over our pyjamas and slipped trainers on. The tent zip sounded deafening in the silence, and I pulled a face at the twins. They tried to smother their giggles. Crawling out of the tent door, we all stood up and stretched, grinning excitedly at each other. The sky was a dim blue colour in the absence of the sun.

'Phew. We haven't missed it. Come on,' I said.

Grabbing one of their hands each, and swinging their arms up and down, we walked away from the campsite and towards the cliff top. Nobody was awake. The cliff, and the beach below, were deserted. We stopped, looking out across the sea, and I closed my eyes, breathing in the salty air. This could be heaven. The waves crashed into the shore, muffled by the gentle wind and height of our position. Such an amazing sound.

'Come on,' Samuel said eagerly. Let's go onto the beach.'

Opening my eyes, I looked down at his excited face and laughed. The steps were steep, so we took our time, but once down on the beach the twins ran towards the distant sea, looking for shells as they went. I followed slowly, drinking in the scene. Every sense was heightened and filled me with pure pleasure. As I looked east, the sun wasn't yet ready to rise. I sat down and watched the children play.

The past two years had been difficult. I had become a patient within the mental health services after the wrist-cutting incident, and I had attended psychiatrist appointments, plus group and individual therapy. At first, I had found it unbearable. Opening up wasn't easy. But, the groups showed me that I wasn't the only one struggling. Not only that, but there were people functioning normally. They had been where I was, and now they were functioning. That could be me.

I was taught skills about how to cope, and how to deal with triggers. Sometimes they worked, but not always. I gradually cut myself less, until one day I didn't feel the need to. Sometimes I lapsed. But that was OK. It's an illness, and some days would always be hard. But, not every day. Most days were OK. Not singing from the rooftops OK, but still OK. I was functioning again. I owed my life to the various doctors, psychiatric nurses and therapists who had spent hour after hour talking and listening to me. And, I owed my life to my children. They also saved me. I couldn't leave them.

Samuel was coping much better on his medication. His dose had been increased and school had become less of an emotional challenge. With the help of his learning support staff, he was excelling in all subjects. Some days were still hard. Just like for me. But, not every day. That's mental health for you.

Robin moved on, and somehow, as the years passed, I did too. He remained my best friend, and we talked often, but it was never the same. I often wondered if he knew how much I still loved him. I had survived, though, and I knew that I would be OK on my own. And he was still my rock. He always would be. I just knew that I was strong enough to hold myself up at last. Losing Robin had broken me. But, it was Robin who also helped to save me. His continued friendship and support kept me alive. I never truly understood our complex relationship, and suspected that I never would.

*

The sky was starting to burn orange and pink on the horizon. I got up excitedly.

'Mia. Samuel. Come here, quickly.'

They ran back towards me, checking over their shoulders towards the sky which had turned a vivid pink. Chattering non-stop, they stood either side of me and I put my arms around them. As the bright orange tip of the sun pierced through the sky, I squeezed their shoulders, and we stood in silence. Tears started to run down my face. I let them. They were happy tears. This wasn't heaven. This was life. My life. Everything I had ever wanted. And I was happy to be alive.

Yes. I was happy.

Printed in Great Britain
by Amazon